DEADLINE FOR FINAL ART

Also written and illustrated by Jan Adkins

DEADLINE FOR FINAL ART

JAN ADKINS

Walker and Company
New York

First published in the United States of America in 1990
by Walker Publishing Company, Inc.

Published simultaneously in Canada by Thomas Allen & Son
Canada, Limited, Markham, Ontario

Library of Congress Cataloging-in-Publication Data
Adkins, Jan
Deadline for final art / Jan Adkins
p. cm.
ISBN 0-8027-5759-6
I. Title.
PS3551.D52D44   1990
813'.54—dc20   90-11968
CIP

Printed in the United States of America
2 4 6 8 10 9 7 5 3 1

To my sister,
JUDY
who is kind and generous
and patient with her often
preoccupied brother.
She leads me beside the still waters.

$\triangledown$

Chapter 1

CHARLIE SALT WAS DREAMING in color. He would have been disappointed with black-and-white.

Outside, the man in the Chevrolet was irritable and tired. He had drunk too much coffee, but he wanted another cup. No damned good for his heart. He should exercise more, too. Now this late-night stuff. Young guys ate it up, but he was past that.

He looked at his nightsheet for Salt. Lights out between twelve and one. Three nights out of seven, lights on again in bedroom and kitchen around five. Subject observed drinking what appeared to be orange juice and talking to himself.

Talking to himself. What about? The man in the Chevrolet wondered only briefly. Not his line of business. Bill's Outfit would figure it.

He looked around his car at an elm-arched street in northwest D.C.. Stable, safe enough to walk for coffee, stop behind a bush to pee, and get back. He followed Outfit policy, opened the briefcase and slipped the handle-taped S & W .38 into his waistband, the silencer into his coat pocket; never leave a car with a piece in it. He locked the nightsheets and photos in the briefcase and opened the door. The dome-light switch was taped down and the door latch was well-oiled. There was a 7-Eleven on Wisconsin where a Vietnamese family was hustling all night. The leaves were beginning to fall, and there was a new chill every Washingtonian welcomes. He walked as briskly as he could, balancing the virtues of exercise against the sins of coffee.

Charlie Salt was dreaming about his wife. In color, in the falling leaves. Their sound came into his dream as they rustled across the porch roof under his window. Kim ran through the brightly dead leaves, her freckles grinning a thousand times, eyes huge and brown, body small and graceful but muscled in the shoulders and arms and in her dancer's front-swelling thighs. She began to unbutton her wind-billowing shirt. She looked devilish and playful.

The dream went on, and this would be one of the mornings Charlie would walk down to the kitchen between five and six to drink juice. He would wake up crying.

He was a block from the Chevrolet, carrying a foam cup of coffee, large, when old sensors lit up in his head. What is it? Something wrong, goddammit. Something out of pattern. He continued to walk, but slowed his pace and unbuttoned his jacket discreetly. At the corner, he crossed. *Circle*, he told himself, *circle in.*

A small black man, neatly dressed in dark colors, came out of the alley behind Salt's house. *Damn, damn, damn,* he thought to himself, *not here, you son of a bitch, go climb in a window anywhere else but here.*

"Evening." Salt nodded.

The black man walked past and answered, "Fine, just fine," in a soft black patois.

He walked thirty yards until the black man had turned the corner, then ran back to the alley. No one in sight. He set the coffee cup down at the end of the alley and moved along the dimmest side, low and fast. Now he knew what his sensors had picked out: a van, Dodge, dark, with commercial lettering on the side. It hadn't been there when he'd left, and this wasn't delivery time. This was pickup time. Pick up silver, pick up CD decks, pick up VCRs. He paused on one knee, fitting the silencer to the .38's short barrel. His orders were clear: No disturbance of any kind around the subject. A burglary on the block or, Jesus, in Salt's home, would red-flag anything the outfit did later.

Up again and moving, soft-soled shoes finding their places,all the old training tumbling out of the box. Fat and old, coffeed-out heart, *But I can still do the dance.*

He approached the end of the alley cautiously. The van was closed, windows up but some movement inside. One of the rear doors opened, and he could see two men, one the polite young man he'd met on the other side of the block. the other was a heavy, jowled man. From the shadows he could hear the heavy man's voice grate like a brush for cleaning concrete. Young Dapper stepped down, stuffing something in his waistband, probably a jimmy, maybe a blade. He nodded to Fats and closed the door softly on him.

By the time Dapper walked through the leaves littering the corner of the lot, the man from the Chevrolet was hidden in a shrub's tendriled branches, very hard to see, holding the old .38 lightly in both outstretched hands, almost an offering.

The rubbery thump of the silencer had a wheeze in it. The plain ball slug caught Dapper just behind his left ear, nothing dramatic, and the lucky thing was that none of the tools clattered out of his belt as he fell. While Dapper's lower brainstem was still shutting down various functions of secretion and regulation he was being dragged up onto the shallow slope of grass that verged the concrete alley, under the shrub and onto the blossoms, where he was laid prettily out in a somnolent pose. His eyes were closed, his head turned left, one hand under it. The soft shoes vaulted back across the fence.

He'll leave or he'll check. If he leaves, it's less trouble now, more later. If he checks, it's only more lifting. The man from the Chevrolet found a comfortable position under the branches and used it, waiting with the piece held up beside his cheek. He could smell the fresh sulfur tang from its one shot. He was a good waiter.

Fats was a bad waiter. Twenty minutes later, he left the van and stumped across the street, rolling from side to side with his arms outspread for balance and keeping his head on an even keel with motions of his shoulders and what was once his neck.

God. How can you let yourself go like that? I've got a beer belly, but like that? No way! He did not change position but continued to wait, kneeling.

"You motherjive sovbitch," Fats hissed. "Wake up, nigger . . ."And Fats was shifting his ponderous bulk to kick at Dapper when he was distracted briefly by a motion in the bushes. He did not hear the sound of a silencer.

Fats was a problem: 325 pounds of uncooperative dead wheel man stinking of voided fluids, he had to be leaned against the bumper of the van and rolled up into it. It was a disgusting job. Dapper was no problem, very simple. The large bush hid every movement, and it was only two miles across Rock Creek Park to Mount Pleasant, a transitional neighborhood, denser, with a high crime rate. He posed them artfully, left the .38 in Fat's hand (he had the wound for suicide), and locked the van before he walked away. There would be no rigorous investigation. There was a good solid explanation, a tight tale. Lack of powder burns? Perry Mason stuff. He iced the kid and killed himself for his own reasons.

A copy of the police blotter secured by Bill's Outfit made Fats and Dapper cousins. The story on Channel 5 news upgraded them to brothers: "A brother slays his brother and kills himself in a tragic story of city crime. Details at eleven."

He returned to his blue Chevrolet as the sky was paling. He felt younger than he had for years. He could still dance. He recognized the man in the car as one of Bill's staff, and he got in beside him. "Larry," he said, "early morning for you isn't it?"

"You just getting to work?"

"Right. Two burglars later."

"Burglars?"

"About to do Salt's joint. I don't know for what. When I was in there, I didn't see a lot to risk B and E for."

"What about the burglars?"

"I gave 'em dinner."

Larry's facade of command disappeared in his agitation. "You terminated them? Here?"

"Calm, calm, Larry. This is only cold coffee, but you're going to spill it for me. Everything is five by five; it all went down neatly, under cover, and cool. Right now . . ."

"Where are they?"

"That's what I'm telling you, Larry. Come on, will you? They're in their van across the park, over where the cops will find them in two days and read it just like it's laid out. Murder and suicide. No one knows."

"Jesus Christ . . ."

"He doesn't know."

"If this gets back . . ."

"Larry." He was scolding Larry now, telling him what happens when you don't brush your teeth. "When you're in the field, you better be ready to read the situation and act independently, using the case itself and the Outfit's policies as a guide—but only a guide. This was our situation." He held up his hand and counted them off. "Independent action, plausible rationalization, and, as always, security. *Verstehen Sie*, Larry? Do we read the blackboard easily this morning? Now, I would have made more points in there, but I would have had to put my coffee down." He took a sip of the alley-cold coffee. It was terrible, but it tasted good this morning.

Chapter 2

CHARLIE SALT POISED ABOVE the sleeping child. His hands transformed into talons. His teeth grew into long fangs. His voice deepened into Middle European gutturals behind his beard. He dived mercilessly at the child's soft belly. "A-ha! You will be one of the Undead!"

"Sneak attack!" yelped the perfidious child, too suddenly awake. Two squirt guns came up from under the blanket, and the beard was sodden, ears dripping at the lobes.

"You little bastard!"

"Yup." He grinned, a rubbery face and several hundred freckles taking gleeful part.

"Look at me, I'm all . . . wet. Ear to ear. What a damn shame. And me about to kiss your tummy!" A dive, shrieks, and misdirected squirts, one pattering against the regal form of The Daughter, descending from her attic room wearing long johns, two towels, and unlaced hunting boots.

The two men outnumbering her in representation and had, thereby, the right to leave the toilet seat up, looked into the hall from their tangle. Charlie commented, "Like your outfit."

Hers was the face of a woman whose last Rolls-Royce has been stolen by peasants who cannot drive, a deep and traveled disgust from someone who knows what a bummer the world can really, swear to God, be. "You two"—she indicated their presence with a flick of her wrist—"are so perverted. Really. Like, a bunch of homos."

"Schottsie," Charlie asked his fellow pervert, "are we . . . homo?"

"Alphonse,"Mike replied, "kees me!"

Loud smacking, more tangling.

"Oh, my God." Sarah stalked into the bathroom.

Charlie got up. Mike clung to him. "Get off me, you pervert. Feet on the floor, get dressed, school stuff together, dirty clothes picked up and all the way to the basement. See you looking sharp and scrubbed in twenty minutes in the kitchen. Lunches to be made, breakfast to be consumed."

He set him on the floor. "You're getting too big to heft around, sport."

"No, I'm not."

"Time to force you out of the nest. If I didn't need you in the nest so much." There was too much truth in that for comfort, so Charlie tickled him into a pile of writhing and left the room.

He banged on the hall bathroom door. "In five minutes, I'm going to turn my shower on full hot. Short shower, kid. Move it. Breakfast in eighteen minutes." Protest from within.

He closed his bedroom door behind him. *This room is too much,*he thought,*Salt's idiosyncratic mechanism for hiding out.* The paintings were all by friends. The big bed and its headboard were antiques found in Maine and reworked in his shop. The reading lights had once been cabin lamps aboard *Pendragon,* his uncle's boat. He had taken them out before the wrecker dismantled her. *Good boat,* he thought.

He began to lay out his clothes. Khakis, a deep-blue cotton shirt, blue socks, a braided belt, deck shoes, a black wool tie,

and his brown herringbone jacket. Turning, he caught himself in the mirror. He smirked at the image, taking stock
nevertheless. No, there was nothing remotely heroic in the
mirror. He saw a bald pate surrounded by close-cropped gray
and white hair. A face that carried forty-three years of sun
and worry lines, not unpleasantly, mossed over with a gray
beard. There was undeniably a modest potbelly, but it was
carried adequately by a stocky build. It was the body of a
runner and a tennis player of no extraordinary skill but great
enthusiasm. There were good hands, bluey-browny eyes,
nice ears—*don't forget those, Salt,*—and a smile that was too
self-conscious to look at anymore. He shook his head and
started for his bathroom.

"Hey, babe." He paused at the picture beside the bathroom door. Kim was grinning at something he had just said
four years ago, her freckles were in thickets from the summer
sun, her slender hands were pulling back a set of strands the
wind had laid across her high, grand brow. She was aboard
Pendragon, the last summer for *Pendragon.* And for her.
"Well, kid, the bairnies look good, growing up in wisdom,
stature, and favor with cod and man."

A *Pendragon* joke. Some joke. "They do look good. Look
like you. Sarah's got the moves, Mike's got the deep part.
Okay, he's a little clingy still, he lags in emotional stature,
but he's got heart, babe. He's all heart and smart, like you."
A sour voice in his mind added, *Like you were.* He looked
at the photograph with the same self-consciousness he had
felt with the mirror and felt empty and soiled and overused,
like a pair of rubber garden boots.

The lucky ones believe in God, he thought to himself,
moving on from the lifeless photograph. *The others learn
what a crap shoot life is.*

"So I'm late. I get to be late. I'm going to the office, you're going to school. Mike, change the shirt, it's frayed. Get one of the new oxford cloth shirts and tuck it in. Brush your teeth while you're up there. Do you have your lunch ready? No? Oh, Lord. I thought it got easier after Pampers. Go, go get the shirt and teeth brushed! You've had breakfast? No? Mike! What have you been doing while I've been dressing?"

"He's been bugging me," Sarah replied for him.

"Me? Me? Who got out the pretzels to throw?"

"For my lunch!"

"Stop, stop! Mike, upstairs! Sarah, I swear you are re-tarded . . ."

"He's the retard. Talking dirty."

"Boys his age have to talk dirty."

"I don't see why."

"So they can talk dirty when they're my age. Now move it, sister, make two lunches."

"I'm going to buy my lunch today. He can fix his own retarded lunch."

"Fix it."

"No. He should fix his own."

"Agreed. Get started. Here, I'll help you fix yours, and you work on Mike's."

At the door, he said, "Go, go, get stolen by the Gypsies, take any ride you can get from a stranger, don't look when you cross."

"See you," Mike said, and kissed him.

"You forgot your lunch for the second time. Sarah made it."

"Go ahead, retard. My God." She stayed behind for a moment changing from a sixteen-year-old to the forty-year-old she had been since her mother died. "Dad, look, don't talk to Mom's photograph, okay? Really, she's dead. I love her still, but she's dead. Call Sue or Ginger today, will you? We haven't had any women in the house for too long. It's affecting me. I'm beginning to think about football."

"Jesus."

"See? We're talking serious business here. Bye, see ya."

"See me when?"

"Ah, I don't know, I think I might have something after school tonight. Practice or something." She was walking backward away, down the block after Mike.

"What practice?"

"I don't know, I just . . . see ya." Sixteen again, she turned and ran down the street, pinching Mike savagely on her way past him and then whooping in delight as he gave chase, shirt untucked.

$\triangledown$

Chapter 3

THIS WAS ONE OF the best times of the day for Charlie. He walked toward the Metro through the descent of maple and elm leaves. He liked the trip to work in the morning. He liked it because the filthy phone couldn't noose him with its imperative rings. Another reason he liked his walk to the Metro was that it steeped him in the city. He might as well get into it. The one drawback of his job was its placement. He was not a city boy. He missed his small coastal town and the sound of waves.

The ground rumbled faintly beneath him as six car trains a hundred feet below Albemarle Street scurried through their tunnels.

He rode the escalator down the grandly bored tube and fed his ticket to the gate, which spit it back out at him, a surly approval that was more like a rejection.

The train was crowded. Charlie stood and tried to read a Ross Thomas book but was distracted by the people. Secretaries with gym bags wearing expensive, I don't-come-cheap office dresses over white socks and running shoes. Lawyers in pin-striped suits and gold-rimmed glasses reading the *Wall Street Journal* with a frosty look of quiet outrage. Civil servants, older men with quiet faces and blurred eyes. Young turks wearing three-hundred-dollar silk jackets over 505 Levis and Bally loafers. A family from Idaho who had probably parked their station wagon on a side street near Tenleytown, coming in to see the Air/Space and the monuments, glad faces except the father, who was wondering how to keep everyone together.

Going to work. Most of these riders were clinging to a last bit of private life or boosting themselves over the wall, into the hurly-burly. For Charlie, it was different; his life at home and his life at work were about equally pleasant, equally stressful. Life for him was a continuum, except that it was less lonely at work and he didn't wear a tie at home.

The Metro doors opened on the starboard side at Dupont Circle, and the rush out swept Charlie with it. *I'm too damned polite*, he thought; *I should stand obdurate*. He liked the sound of it in his head: Obdurate Charlie Salt. He reboarded at the piercing electronic chime, thinking, *It won't be long until we have white-gloved pushers packing us like Port Clyde sardines, big guys who didn't make the pro draft, chanting apologies, "Sorry, sorry, 'scuse me, door closin', sorry . . ."* At Farragut North, the door opened and a hundred lawyers squirted out, riding their briefcases toward success. Charlie followed them.

Charlie was more comfortable with sandy roads that had weeds on the berm. He had never, in ten years, accustomed himself to the city. But this was his street, because his job was here, a job he was designed by nature to do. He looked around him and saw faces he knew, faces of colleagues and friends and faces he only recognized. He might not like the city, but he belonged in one building, here.

Turning the corner, he looked up Seventeenth to check the flags. *Damn*. One flag was at half-mast.

Edward Durrel Stone designed the new headquarters of

the National Geographic Society with the same vacuous grandiosity lavished on the Kennedy Center. White marble pillars rise to the D.C. maximum height, ten stories (only the old Cairo escaped through the last loophole and made it to twelve). The columns fin outward with black-curtained wall windows behind them. Undistinguished, stiff, pompous and, like much totalitarian architecture, more impressive at night with the lights. This morning, the American flag to the north of the entrance flew at the mast head, but the Society flag was at half mast. *One of our own has died.* Charlie nodded to himself. He felt diminished for he belonged to the Society as surely as to a continent or a piece of the main. Someday the flag would dip for him.

Until he joined the Society (he did not think of it as being hired), he had belonged to nothing. To a woman, a bay, a piece of terrain. But his fealty was loose. He had kept it that way and thought romantically about the medieval meaning of "free-lance."He had written and illustrated books about how things worked: stories, articles, an eclectic career of explaining things. Now he explained things to eleven million members, forty million readers, making statements that were read in doctors' offices, dentists' waiting rooms, and toilets all over the world. It had crept up on him in ten years that he belonged. It felt good, like a Saturday shirt, or a responsibility enjoyed.

"Marilyn, who bought it?" He stopped at the receptionist's desk and pointed up behind him toward the flag.

"Oh Mr. Salt, one of the guards, Mr. Wheeler, was killed last night by a burglar or a prowler or . . . somebody, I just don't know, I just think . . ." She shook her head; she was close to tears. Wheeler, a tall, genial black man about Salt's age, was often the front lobby guard during the day, a man you passed minutes with waiting for a visitor or a lunch date.

A smiling, firm man. Solid. Marilyn would have come to know him even better.

Charlie leaned over the desk and put his hand over Marilyn's clasped, worrying hands. "He was a nice man, Mr. Wheeler, and he had a good word for all of us. But it happens."

"Not here. It shouldn't happen here. We're not like that, Mr. Salt."

"No. No, but they are, Marilyn, and we're part of them. You want to go wash up or something? I'll hold down the desk for a while."

"No, thank you. I'll stay right here. Thanks, Mr. Salt."

He was about to tell her "Charlie," but he had given it up two years ago. She met the public, and it required her formality. He winked at her and took the next elevator up. It stopped at two and Captain Barry got in.

Fiftyish, large, the captain of the Geographic guards, Barry wore his uniform well and had the wary courtesy of a former motorcycle cop. His speech was usually soft and black, but today it was tightened by something in his throat.

"Captain Barry. I'm sorry about Mr. Wheeler. I know everyone is asking and interfering—"

"Corporal Wheeler. Corporal Wheeler was a fine man. Steady. He would have been on the force with us . . ." he watched the floor numbers rise to keep his eyes on something, ". . .come on to twelve years next month. Steady. You could send a card to his wife. No flowers. Mrs. Wheeler's allergic. Bad business. Here, too."

"Yes, here. What happened? I mean, I don't want to stick my oar in—"

"Found him on the floor, Mr. Salt, in the north stairwell. Windpipe busted. Bad. Some lucky punch from a punk. Nothing taken, but we're still doing inventory. You'll have to go through your things."

They both got out on eight. Captain Barry started away toward the west corridor without a word. Not like him. He stopped at the corner of the elevator bank and turned. "I'll post the address in the cafeteria. You send the card, Mr. Salt. Remember, no flowers. Have a nice day." But he didn't smile.

Charlie walked the corridor in silence, trying to shake off the taint of tragedy before he began work. He hung his bag on the back of the door with his jacket. His office was a mess. It always was. But there was a strange tincture of order. Stacks of reference magazines and books were straighter, the gray bags that collected page layouts for individual stories were filed neatly, his desk was clear though he remembered that something was on it when he went home. What? The pencils were in ranks on his desk. Charlie Salt had a graphic mind; it was his gift. At the beginning of every month, he cleaned his office to anal-retentive order, but this was toward the end of September. He saw, or thought he saw, that the room had been systematically reordered, but a handful of papers had been fluttered onto each surface afterward. It made him curious.

"No. I haven't had a second to do anything this morning." Ruth was the department manager. She tracked the stories and kept the schedules of all art due, research ongoing, supplies, everything. She also remembered birthdays and anniversaries and noticed sad looks and covered for lapses in decorum or timing. She was a good egg and had fluttery feminine mannerisms that would have been a pain in a woman less strong or less good-hearted. "Isn't this just awful . . . I mean awful, Charlie. Mr. Wheeler, right down the hall, and here, right here at the Geographic. My God."

"Yeah, Wheeler." He was still trying to get to work and get away from it. "Who's been in my office, anyway?"

"No one. That I know of. Wait, Ron maybe, getting the

layouts for 'Plains Indians.' Ron," she called up the corridor
to the staff artist, Ron Gould who could duplicate anyone's
illustration style and had a few of his own, "hey, were you
in Charlie's office this morning or late last night?"

"Why'sat? Silver missin'?" Ron was a cockney. It had been
thirty years since he lived in the sound of the Bow bells but
the accent still had its twang and edge. "Well, there I was,
love, creepin' in 'ere in black hat and gloves and such,
coppin' valu'bles, lookin' in Charlie's room for candlesticks
and what, I'm confronted by Constable Wheeler. 'Right,
then,' says he, 'what's all this?' I raises up and I says, 'You'll
never take me alive, screw!' and bash him, bang, dead. It was
me, Ron Gould." He giggled, and clapped a hand to his
mouth, instantly somber. "I shouldn't said that. Terrible
thing, that is. Strike me dead. Poor Mr. Wheeler." Ron Gould
was a wonderfully silly man. It helped him put up with the
Geographic, where a talent like his was the final amulet
against mistakes found too near deadline.

"It's nothing really, about the office, I mean," Charlie
said. "Some elf cleaned it up for me and then made it look
messy. Funny."

Ron always reminded him of deadlines. "Jesus, I just
thought, the 'Airships' story. Have we got the corrections
run on that?"

"Oh, no, y'see Elaine din't give me those till, when was
it, noon yesterday, yes, and I finished 'em up last night at
'ome. Anything wrong?"

"Not if we make an arrangement with brother Keeton. See
you at—Ruth, is scheduling at ten this morning?"

"Oh, yes, death, taxes and scheduling. No golf tourna-
ment, no seminar, no rain or snow or gloom of night.
Scheduling at ten."

Charlie walked up the corridor to the kingdom of Printing

and Engraving: a hall, or what Stone's design module would
allow for a hall, centering a great table, seven by twenty-four,
on which the uncut sheets of proofs were laid and marked.
Under the surface were a hundred flat drawers for proofs and
art. Handing over final art to Printing and Engraving was
something delicate, a moment of nerves, like handing over
your ship to the canal pilot's authority, your child to the first
grade school bus. Charlies's life was goosed and jerked back
by the magazines's changing schedules, but there were
deadlines and deadlines. There was the deadline that was
printed weekly, revealed at scheduling, the nominal deadline
that you hewed to. Then there was late date, time for
revisions (and decisions which a minute will reverse). Then
there was the drop-dead date. After that, there was trouble,
trouble and money in six figures.

At the end of the long table stood Bill Keeton, a thin dark
suit topped by a shock of white hair and beard. He was
peering dyspeptically at a black loose-leaf notebook that
contained the printing schedules, the Real Stuff—routing
orders for tons of paper, overtime approval for hundreds of
printers, glitches, holidays, labor problems. Keeton's eyes
had acquired, over twenty-five years, a cast of doom. He
looked up at Salt's face. "Oh, no," he said, the dark of his
suit in his voice, "what's gone wrong?"

"Wrong?" Charlie replied brightly. "What could go wrong?"

"Sunrise," Keeton replied with certainty.

"Airships."

"Late." One eyebrow elevated another notch. "How late?"

"Just done. Needs final pass by research."

Keeton smiled sardonically. "Final pass. Ha. Let's look at
the 'Doomsday Book'." He flipped through the pages. "Due
in Corinth yesterday. Mmm. Tight."

"What can you give me?"

Keeton put the book down at the very edge of the bowling alley table. He peered at it, trying to squeeze an answer out of it with his eyes. He opened his jacket and hitched his thumbs behind red suspenders. All right, Charlie thought, he was willing to deal. They were out in front of the general store now. "Truth is, we're held up on cutting cylinders by some hitch in Corinth." Corinth, Mississippi, the printing plant that spun out eleven million copies of the magazine every month with minimum wastage and maximum flexibility of time and change. The president of the Society sent presents every year: bonuses, improvements, golf tournaments, and a full circus for employees and families every fall. "I could slip this in with some difficulty."

"Perhaps I can help you down the line."

"Yes, you could. On 'Milky Way Galaxies,' a lot of dropout type in that?"

White lettering dropped out of a black background, it was a problem of making all four passes of the press overlap perfectly. If the images slipped a quarter of a millimeter the white edges would "rainbow," with overlapping red, blue, and yellow at the edges.

"Worse." Charlie held his palms up, "Hand lettering. Artist is Lacey Ingalls."

"Aah." A derisive sound. Keeton esteemed no artist but one. The rest, including Rembrandt and the whole Renaissance, were trouble. "Can you get the lettering on a separate overlay, not on the art, approved by the Sioux women *b for* nominal deadline?" The Sioux women were the researchers; they came after the battle with small knives to dispatch the weak in amusing ways.

"I can do that."

"Can you make it type instead of hand lettering?"

"I can consider it and consult with the artist."

"We can do hand stuff if you absolutely need it, but I'd sooner use type Karl can set in-house when the corrections come."

"I'll see if it works in."

"Good enough. And the corrections. No one but Ron." The Artist.

"No one. The magic touch."

"Friday. If we have 'Airships' by Friday, we won't sweat. Now, is the original with us?"

"Ron should have put it in here this morning."

Keeton went down the table looking at month labels on the flat drawers. "Here we go. April. Should be in here, but who the hell knows. Someone rearranged the drawers for us last night. Got things out of sequence. Don't know who."

"Funny," Charlie said, thinking about something else and heading for the stairwell to the Research floor.

Inspector Carlton Deauville stood in the stairwell and chewed a toothpick. His mind was idly scrolling through facts. He was resting.

Wheeler, the deceased, was a forty-nine-year-old black male. Security guard. Five-nine, one hundred and sixty-five pounds, scars above right eye. Trachea crushed by a blow. Minor head wounds in the fall down three steps.

Scenario: Night prowler rummaging for valuables on the eighth floor is surprised by Wheeler in the stairwell. A fight ensues as Wheeler tries to apprehend. A chance blow crushes Wheeler's windpipe, and the prowler leaves as Wheeler spends an uncomfortable five or ten minutes dying.

The victim's outline had been chalked on the stairs. Deauville could see Wheeler from where he stood as though he were still there. A thin black man lying three steps down against the wall, trying to pull in enough plain air to live.

Lying with his head down the stairs, mostly unconscious, confused and, finally, gone.

He should leave. He had other cases.

Carlton Deauville had been a policeman for twenty years. He was a careful man. He used his money wisely and had a little real estate business on the side. He had avoided being married long enough to make a good catch. He had gotten himself a wife fine-looking enough to make him—if not pussy-proof—at least pussy-resistant. He didn't truck in deals or drugs or ladies. He liked his captain well enough and had gotten over the inevitable ulcer. Life was not a pain to him. He could sit waiting to testify in court and think about his wife or houses he could buy in Arlandria or where they could go on vacation. Even if she couldn't cook worth a damn, she was something, all right. With a body like that and a good business head, she was a piece of goods.

So why didn't he leave?

Because Wheeler had been a boxer. Not just a boxer but lightweight champion of the Seventh Cavalry in 'Nam. It didn't go down right with Deauville: even years after and pounds heavier, you don't hit a good fighter in the windpipe with a lucky punch.

He handled thirty new homicides every month, most of them suicides and suspicious deaths and drug deals gone sour, domestic disturbance and barfight victims. He had learned to accept a lot of chance and coincidence. An occasional wild card was no reason to hold up paperwork. But Carlton didn't trust chance. He was a peevish, suspicious man who looked inside every sandwich he ever bit. He didn't like Corporal Wheeler's death by chance blow.

The stairwell door opened, and Charlie came in. The two men looked at each other without speaking for a time. *Man needs an ironing board*, Carlton said to himself, looking at

Charlie's rumpled khakis. He had already made a stack of mental notes on Salt: unmarried or separated; forty to forty-five, still works out, five-nine or ten, one ninety; no rings or jewelry, but a blue twill shirt with a black tie, showy; expensive pen, technical pencil, sheaf of telephone messages in shirt pocket; unpolished expensive shoes with Vibram thinsoles, worn, a walker; hands won't stay still—man's got a worry.

"Hi." Charlie looked down the stairs to the outline and back to the black man with a gold detective's shield hanging from his jacket pocket.

The black man nodded slowly, looking out from under his hat brim. "You work here? On this floor?"

Charlie nodded, pointing over his shoulder at the door to the eighth floor. The he looked back at the bloodstain that remained. "Right there?" he asked.

The detective nodded calmly, as if death and mayhem happpened every day for him. Of course, it did.

"I'm Charlie Salt. I'm the associate art director for the magazine. 852." He pointed to the door again. Like all talkative men, Charlie filled the silence for quiet men. "I knew Officer Wheeler, but not very well. Just to say hello.

Another slow nod, but no effort to reach up and shake hands, introduce himself.

"Are you investigating the . . . death? Accident?"

"Murder, maybe. Carlton Deauville, Homicide. You know anything about this?"

"Zero. I wish I knew something."

"You probably don't. Wish you do, that is. Unless you like trouble more than most. If you do think of something, any little thing, you know? Get in touch with me. Here's my card. Got two little numbers down here you can reach me all the time."

"You bet, yessuh. Thanks." Charlie continued down the stairs, skirting past the chalked outline and past the unmoving Deauville.

One floor down and north along to the corridor of Research. It was quiet here. Even with the occasional group of researchers proofing to one another, reading aloud in soft tones. He had fifteen minutes before scheduling. Marilyn Gallidet was bending over sheaf of notes and cross checking them with a stack of green copy proofs. "Airships."

"Marilyn, we've corrected all the inconsistencies on the art and released it to P and E. Just wanted to check in with you, darlin' "

Marilyn shook her head at the proofs. Charlie's stomach dropped, and he reached for the imaginary pistol he carried for Philistines. "We've got an anachronism here. You've shown the Goodyear with twenty gores of outer skin. That's with the new wide looms at Ravenswood." What the hell did Charlie care about goddamned Ravenswood? He pulled his pistol and cocked the hammer. "At the time we show it, 1954, they were using the old narrower fabric. Thirty-six gores. Has to be changed."

"Come on, Marilyn, you can hardly see the seams in Ron's painting."

"Then how could I count the gores? It's wrong." There was no apology here. None expected. It was an old system, ancient. Adversary research. Art department researchers dug out the information for Charlie and the artist; editorial research did their work independently and tried to prove them wrong. Their honor lay in . . . what? Finding mistakes? Sometimes it seemed like that. Charlie uncocked the big Philistine horse pistol and put it away. Their honor lay in getting the sonofabitch unimpeachably right. Somewhere out there among forty-five million readers was an expert, maybe a hundred, on the goddamned gores of Goodyear blimps. Okay. "Right, Marilyn, good work. Run those boogers down, you sharp-eyed little terrier. We'll change the gores late this morning. Anything else?"

"Only the typeface on the numbers. They shouldn't be italic, just roman, straight-up-and-down stuff." She smiled over her little victory.

Charlie smiled back. "Nasty bitch. You've saved my ass again. You have a copy of the specs? A memo?"

She handed him a Xerox of the memo already prepared, already copied to the editor-in-chief, and smiled again. She had a nice smile, and she was good; she knew it this morning. Actually, she was an attractive woman, pleasingly mammalian.

The old door, four years old, slammed. "Thanks, pal." He took the memo and jogged up the corridor to the other stairwell, forgetting about Marilyn's jugs.

Charlie jogged up to Ruth's desk where Ron was gossiping. "Ron, skip scheduling and change the number of gores on the goddamned Goodyear blimp. Here's a memo from the research mavens."

"Coo. Lot they know about it." Ron's face went pouty. He was disappointed not to be with the big boys in scheduling.

"Ruth, I've got five minutes. Do I have an art schedule? Do I have any tidbits that will come up?"

"If something comes up on the 'Predator Spiders,' we have sketches in from Jack Unruh. Very fine . . ." Ruth made a chef's circle with thumb and finger.

"I should have seen them."

"You were too busy."

"Okay. On the 'Virginia Glory' wreck . . ."

"We're tracking the story." Elaine, one of the art researchers, spoke up behind him. She had a voice like a cracked stilletto from a frame like a stilletto's sheath, a transplanted Wyoming girl with eating disorders of some persuasion, but smart.

"Tell me about 'tracking.' "

The illustrator, Ken Dallison, has the research package and will send back sketches next week."

"You mean . . ."

"With Ken? In good time. He'll call."

"Keep on him. Jolly him up. Send him an atlas."

"He has an atlas."

"Threaten his dog, his cat."

"I can do that."

"I know you can. You're good at . . ."

"Scheduling?" Ruth reminded them.

"I'm off. Where's the Boy?"

"In his office."

"I'll pick him up."

Murray was hunched over a thick tome as though it were Mad Magazine. "Come on, Skeeter, brief me on the space defense story on the way up; I didn't get a chance to read your big memo last night. Mike had a paper we had to write."

"Is that legal?"

"Space defense?"

"No, writing Mike's papers. But as it turns out, neither one is really legal by the letter of the law because . . . Here, get this elevator . . ."

"Just helping the little bastard with some spelling, a little editing, so's he can make sense . . ."

"That's what he's there to learn, and it's none of my concern. But pumping up X-ray lasers with nuclear fission devices into orbit is an international no-no, because of mutually agreed upon treaties. Strictly forbidden, and any-

way the lasers are not so impressive as a defense against the
expected Soviet array of ten to the fourth Vipers . . ."

"Slow down, Skeeter. Ten thousand-plus incoming
rockets . . ."

MIRVs, decoys, balloon shelters, a cast of characters that
would fill up the Ithaca lacrosse stadium. I talked the piece
through with a friend of mine at the Pentagon yesterday,
Wally Tripp. By the way, where did you get your picture of
that warhead?"

"Hold it, you showed the layout to the Pentagon? Skeeter . . ."

"No coach, wave off. Wally's an old friend, a *canpañero*,
old Cornell man. We used to date the same girl, Betty
Burnell. Male bonding, coach. No, he gave me a reading and
ran it up the line a piece to his boss, who's in some
intelligence splinter, and we'll get some feedback soon.
Colonel Bill Brunzell and his Outfit. They run maverick
projects for . . . I don't know who, for someone in the
alphabet soup over there."

"Enthusiasm. That's wha you're good for, Skeeter. But
you fucked up. We don't show new layouts until they're
approved. Comprende? No big deal, but it makes the line
of approval neater and cleaner for the Sioux women to
follow. No big deal. We'll get word back from these guys,
anyway?"

"Oh, sure. Sorry, coach."

"Hey, no damn big. Get to work on that Bahamian wreck
site today and get me the best scanning electron micropho-
tographs of a nerve cell for the Brain Chemistry piece. That's
going to jump up and bite us in the ass if we don't get some
work done on it. Okay?"

"Okay, big fellah. And where did you get that warhead?"

"That? Oh, hell, it's something I saw through a door at

Lawrence Livermore Labs. Probably a weather satellite or something but it stuck in my mind and it fit the bill. Any spinach on my teeth?"

"You look great, except for the boogers."

"Thanks, kid. Fuck off."

Charlie went down the hall to scheduling.

In a great cathedral or a Bedouin tent or a union hall, the feature attraction is raised before the faithful. In this way, the scheduling sessions were puzzling. He Who Must Be Obeyed, the editor-in-chief, John Wheeler Stone, entered late while his minions and lieutenants milled about for coffee at the urn. When he sat—in the one gold chair in the front row—all sat. But he would twist his chair briefly, impatiently and rise again. He would tell the thirty editors about the practical news—the Society infighting that affected them—and about news from the field. Then he would sit again and address not the thirty men and women behind him but the Big Board, the computer-projected schedule of stories cast on the wall before him with their dates and mixes per issue. Each issue was to be a meal of varied offerings: natural history, technology, human interest, pure science. Each issue was a theme with contrasting flavors. Each issue was Stone's, and his stamp was on every legend, every photo selection, every layout, every painting and illustration, every map. He spoke to the wall as a Mayan priest might explain the daily world of his village to local gods. John Wheeler Stone told stories to the wall, about what he'd done that week, and how his vines were growing, and how the legends on "Veldt Giraffes" needed work, and how the president of the Society was delighted about the renewal rate and . . . What was the rate this week?

Mary Ann, at the left of the green, quivering wall today, answered, "Eighty-five point four five percent. A little below last year's at this time, but we haven't sent out our renewal mailer yet. We expect results from that."

The big head nodded: Yes, yes. Mary Ann continued but was stilled with a hand, and a new subject was voiced to the wall, "Is Ali Boutou, that sonofabitch, going to come through with the goddamned manuscript in time for next Easter or next Fourth of July, or should we just write the little crook off and let him stew out there? Buy him off with five bucks and a bouquet?" He voiced this suggestion to no one, but it was addressed precisely.

The modulated tones of the unruffelable contract editor, Charles McCarry, replied, "I thing we should send out a contract on him. We'd get the manuscript in five days."

Laughter, but not from the Stone. "Why do we want to kill him? We want the words. He's been out there for ten months, Mac."

"He's in Morocco. A contract on his life would ensure his good health, but he'd know we meant business."

Titters, but not from the Stone. "See if a phone call or a cable or a diverted photographer or something will convince him of our seriousness. Or else give him whatever and start fresh. Got that?"

"Yes, Jack." Unruffled, but convinced.

"How's photo coverage on 'Piedmont?' "

The director of photography, lean and deadpan, a man who had an electric guitar and a stuffed sheep in his office, spoke somberly, "Jim will be bringing his last rolls in on Thursday, and when his hangover subsides on Sunday afternoon, we'll take a look at it together."

"One week, then. Monday." People wrote Monday down in their daybooks.

"Is Harold here?"

He was asking for the art director, a rhetorical question.

The art director, known as the White Rabbit, ran so many projects in so many directions for every part the the Society but the magazine that his mind could only be had for fragments of afternoons. Harold was Charlie's boss, and at one time was the smartest, wiliest, finest graphic mind on the East Coast. But in twenty-six years Harold had won and shelved his spurs, on to bigger, broader projects, keeping the title against the Flood, against the occasional earthquake or disaster. He could pick out the inconsistency in a legend or the repetitive pattern in three successive layouts, almost as reliably as the Stone, but the White Rabbit was seldom there to do it.

"Not present but accounted for," Charlie answered him, logically, as associate art director.

"Charlie?"

"Yo."

" 'Space Defense.' How are we going to deal with all those MIRVs?"

How did the fucker do it? How did he keep his fingers in so many pies?

"I've got a layout working that will show you."

"Good."

Another voice. "We also have a cartographic solution that may make a little more sense with so many reentry vehicles, Jack." Mervin Lighter, the design head of Cartography, Charlie's competition in page design and explanation.

"The maps won't show the types of missles used or the delivery systems . . ."

"A minor point, Charlie. We can pull them out to the side and show them better . . ."

"Work this out in the layout room," said Stone. "Charlie, see me in my office after scheduling." It could be a rebuke or a promotion. Probably neither. It was more likely the lights on the Stone's tennis court.

"You want to get beat this weekend?"

"Yeah, but she canceled out. I thought I'd play some tennis."

"Okay, how about early? We'll clean up the vineyard in the morning, then play in the afternoon. You got a partner for doubles?"

"Not for a while."

"Well, Martha's come up with a woman from State Department. Good looker, supposedly a good player. If she can't play, we can just insult her. Bring the kids, if you want. We'll pay Mike to be ballboy and wise off."

"Saturday morning. You got it." He turned to go.

"Hey. You've got to be more diplomatic or some damned thing about Cartographic. They're doing a hell of a job."

"They used to do a hell of a job under Harold, who has taste."

"They still do, and get it done faster. Harold Dorfler has a lot on his plate. I don't know what all of it is but it must be important. I guess. Patch up the fence. Make it neat, at least. Saturday morning. Maybe we'll have time to put up the lights."

"Saturday morning. Get your backhand out of the closet."

"Ruth, get me a sangy when you go down, will you? Chicken salad with sprouts on pita. Low residue on the drafting board. Get Murray in here after his lunch, take my calls, and buy yourself a Jaguar sedan on me. You're a goddamn pearl above price."

She fluffed her hair like the subject of a 1930s *New Yorker* cartoon. "Just a working girl, but dedicated to the cause." She held out one hand which was missing a cigarette holder. He should get her a damned cigarette holder; it would scandalize the eighth floor. He liked the eighth floor a little off balance.

Time for some work. He put on his Winsor & Newton apron and turned on his radio. He laid out the crabbed parameters of the magazine's sizes and columns in 4H pencil, light on cold press Strathmore. You might as well go first class. Of course, he could have gone D'Arches, but he was frugal first class.

He pulled the rough sketch out of the "Distant Sensing" gray bag where he had been comparing some research. He shook his head; what if someone needed it? Even Murray would have a hard time finding it. It was a black-and-white pencil sketch, its tones roughed in with charcoal, always the prettiest; the final seemed stiff against it. He propped it up against his colored pencils, forty-eight vibrant colors—count them if you have the time, which he didn't.

He pulled out a dozen gray folders and their reference files, because this layout had been an effort of synthesis. It happened sometimes. You worked on ten years of science and technology stories and they began to key in to one another.

Charlie knew from interviews with aerospace engineers at the Lawrence Livermore Labs that any effective missile deterrent system had to be directed by early detection. That meant a constellation of satellites that skimmed low over the Plesetsk, Turyatam, and Baikonur launch sites. He knew their location and launch trajectories from "Soviet Space". He knew the satellites skimming low over the eastern hemisphere would rebound high over the west, and he could generalize the orbits they would assume to give full-time coverage of Soviet launch activity. So far, so good. He drew the orbits in.

The information from the satellites would be passed by

Defense Information Strengthened Command Units, DIS-
CUS (he was familiar with this system from "Those Useful
Satellites"), to the Defense Air Command Center in Colo-
rado, which would land line it to Washington and analysis
center in Pennsylvania and Virginia, and get a command
decision.

Then what? Where did the tactical information go? One
logical assumption was that the information would be fed
to satellites on regular low-orbit launch codes with blue-
green lasers. These lasers could penetrate a hundred meters
of ocean and communicate with submerged boomer—picket
missile subs running silent. Charlie still had all his research
from "Amazing Lasers" and "Submarines Today, Fast
Friends Under."

And the deterrent? It had to be a pop-up missile fired from
a normal Trident tube. There was no problem with the size
of the missile: its diameter and length would fit the launch
tubes described in *Aviation Weekly*. The missile would climb
to a fairly high altitude—outside of the earth's atmosphere—
before performing, and there Charlie's guesswork edged in.
Only one of the weapons the Pentagon briefs mentioned
could strike sufficiently quickly and effectively, given all the
information processed by satellite and ground sources, weed-
ing out decoys and later-blooming packets of MIRVs. A
fission-pumped X-ray laser.

It was Charlie's dictum that they published only a tenth
of what they researched. Among the research detritus of
"Amazing Lasers" were conversations held at Lawrence
Livermore and Los Alamos on fission lasers. The discussions
had never been verified by phone and had never gone through
research checking by the Sioux women because the subjects
simply didn't apply to the "Lasers" text. As Murray had said,
deploying the nuclear lasers was probably against agree-

ments and treaties. But who the hell knew what the treaties really said?

One trip to Lawrence Livermore Labs in California was particularly clear in Charlie's mind. He was walking in a security area with two physicists. They were saying that an enormous source of energy was needed to create a destructive beam that could span long distances and destroy in a millisecond. The only possibility that could be boosted quickly into orbit was a nuclear fission bomb that could pump the energy of the sun's core into computer-aimed laser tubes in the nanosecond before the entire package consumed itself. The result would be a fierce fan of high-energy beams—photons at X-ray frequencies, wire-thin and broadening only a little over hundreds of thousands of miles. When they met any material in the vacuum of low earth orbit, they would transfer their energy intact, in a searing pulse of pure heat that would scramble electronic systems, negate electronic countermeasures, and explode the shaped charges in the warheads and anything else they touched.

Of course, such a laser defense system would cause atomic explosions above the earth's atmosphere. There would be an initial pulse of radiation to anyone below the charge, and then an unpredictable toxic fallout. How many missiles would be fired? How many would it take to assemble a shell of radioactive waste around the planet? How widely would the initial energy pulse harm humans, animals, the rain forests, the surface-dwelling ocean algae? How would the background count go up? No one knew. That was why nuclear explosions in orbit were forbidden by mutual treaty between all nations.

But Charlie's job was to explain. Personally, Charlie did not believe that stockpiles of nuclear weapons had created the *Pax Hiroshima*. He thought armies were like booze:

inevitable, dangerous, and mind-altering. He thought every
general should be given nifty tanks and interesting weapons
to fool around with and to swat small fires, but he did not
trust anyone with the responsibilities of a ten-megaton
device. His mandate, though, was not to moralize but to
explain the facts. If a broad perimeter must be defended
against incoming missiles, only an X-ray laser on a pop-up
missile was effective and hardy. An orbital platform, even
one capable of radical orbit changes, was a slow-moving,
predictable target. His research on this story and ten other
related stories, his conversations with astrophysicists and
with his main aero-astro source, Piggy Holmes, had convinced him that the X-ray laser—interesting from a physics
standpoint—would, at least, be considered. Charlie doubted
it would ever get beyond the consideration point, because no
real test of such a radical weapon was possible. If his readers
understood just how dangerous this orbital alternative was,
Charlie had done his job, as thoroughly as possible. Every
orbit height, every submarine class, every dimension and
distance should be as close as he could reference, deduce, or
estimate.

What was the project called? He remembered the day he
had seen the odd satellite cannister at Livermore; a physicist
was rattling on about something similar and being stopped
by a black look from his colleague. What was the name? He
needed a title.

He laid in the dark indigo sky over a Prussian blue ocean.
Should have had Ron Gould airbrush it in for him, but the
chalks would do for a presentation sketch. It was messy
fingerwork—kindergarden stuff—that Charlie liked. He
blended the colors of the sea, changing the hue and light as
it crossed from east to west. Now he scribed in the coastline
with a hardly detectable colored line—a neatline—that made

it look precise, and scumbled in warm colors on the land. It didn't look like that from the shuttle, but it was Charlie's job to explain, not to duplicate. With an electric eraser, he cleaned the edges of the layout where the chalk had smudged outward, then sprayed it with workable fixative. He worked in some relief on the continents with colored pencils and then picked out the ghost of the missile sub under the surface of the ocean with a kneaded eraser. Charlie worked with patience, lea ned from Ron Gould and parenting.

Now some threat missiles in the sky, streaking across the Soviet border in white opaque paint laid down with a sable brush and just enough water to make them ghostly. When they dried they were too ghostly, and Charlie laid in another wash.

Patience. The chicken salad with sprouts in pita lay uneaten, unnoticed.

He drew the missile erupting from the boomer and breaching in a burst of sea froth. Then the first-stage burn, the second, and the fiery lance arched toward the reader.

Charlie used a straight edge to lay down dotted, color-coded lines to and from color-coded satellites. Some of them were real satellites from research scrap; some were good guesses. He patched in an insert box of the fission missile itself. . . . What was it's name?

He looked at the tracing-paper sketch of how he thought the warhead had to look. He had thought of the orbital package he had seen for a few seconds through an open door at Livermore. Charlie's package would be about the same diameter, and would have the same transparent dome. Half unconsciously Charlie drew the Livermore object—it looked . . . right. He gave the warhead a fall-away shroud, aimable tubes, and navigation parts. He drew in a small cutaway to the nuclear device within. He striated the last stage for shell-stiffness and because it looked good. Designers had prerogative even if weapons-designers didn't. He laid in a crisp rendering of the infernal machine in color; the first sketch had been accurate but not as dramatic.

He used the electric eraser and colored pencils to draw in the second line of defense—shipboard railguns—and the land-based third line of particle-beam defenses with their generating plants beside them.

He looked at it, still taped to his drafting table. Did he believe it?

It didn't matter, but no, he didn't. He didn't want eight or ten or a hundred of these nasty little bastards going off over his head to preserve Ford Motor Company and Beatrice Foods. He knew that the detection and deterrent precentage could be an admirable 85 percent, if absolutely nothing went wrong. Fifteen percent of what the paranoid old buffaloes threw at us out of the U.S.S.R. was way too much for him. It was enough to throw the Geographic vacation schedule right to hell. But it was his job to explain things. Did it explain it? Yes.

Ruth had gone home and the sketch was done. What was the name of the bastard? All he could remember was "Dauphain" so he lettered a headline: "Dauphain, Controversial Prince of Defense." He was bad at titles, but Mike would want to eat. There was a good clear column to explain things, some space for notes. But if Harold had taught him anything, it was to keep his notes simple and compact. He would take the piece home with him and look at it a few times. Maybe he could come up with another slant. Italian sausages and pasta should help; it would help Mike, at least.

He didn't have time to walk forty-five minutes up Connecticut and through the neighborhoods, so he took the

Metro again. As he walked to the Farragut North stop, the blue Chevrolet hung back, its driver watching the jaunty spring in Charlie Salt's step. He looked as if he had just gotten laid.

But, to Charlie, finishing a good layout was almost better than getting laid. Probably because he didn't remember what getting well laid by an attentive lover felt like. There was spring in his step, all right. Salt was a man whose body language presented everything in him, a neon sign, a bad poker player. So to the the driver of the blue Chevrolet, a close and controlled man, Charlie's flamboyance was confusing.

The man in the Chevrolet was hung up by an accident ahead of him on Eighteenth. He should have taken Fifteenth. Charlie bounced into his own door before the driver was on station at Tentleytown. Damn. He would call in for orders from the Outfit.

Chapter 4

"No, you can't do your homework down here. Study habits. Harvard, Cornell, Princeton, Ohio State. In your room, at your desk."

What said he had to be consistent? Sometimes he liked to have them downstairs with him while he fixed dinner. Sometimes he liked to be alone.

He took a cold mug out of the freezer and poured himself the last Tusker, a lovely African lager with the wild taste and smell of hops strong in it. He tossed off a third and let it settle his mouth and throat. Roll down, roll down Jordan. *Beer is for quaffing,* he told himself, *not for sipping.*

He had sweet sausage and marinara from Vace, the Italian deli on Connecticut. He laid them out with garlic and a yellow onion and mushrooms. He washed the mushrooms in his colander. *I should brush the bastards with a fussy little brush and keep them dry,* he thought, *but I haven't got the patience.* He used the big Calfalon skillet, poured in enough olive oil to skim the face, and let it heat slowly. The big Henckels French cook's knife needed rebeveling in his shop, but the edging on the steel would see him through the onion. He sliced it thin, with the same pleasure his skill at the drawing board gave him. *I am not the best cook in the city, but I love it as much.* Kate loved to sit at the end of the big cutting board, four by six, and watch him cook while she sipped her—

Another old door in his head slammed as he picked the rings of onion off the board with the flat of the blade and slid them into the fragrant oil. *What next, what next?* he asked himself.

Greens, steamed vegetables from last night, scallions, chilled hearts of palm in Henckeled rounds, all in the salad bowl. He put the sausage around the perimeter of the skillet to brown slowly. The garlic he minced with quick strokes and mashed with the side of the knife, then mixed it with the onions. Was there ever enough garlic? Not this side of the Styx. Olivewood tongs to turn the sausage, and another jolt of Tusker.

Something was bothering him, some pattern within the pattern, like a "river" in set type, a diagonal slash of spaces that made a jarring stripe of white in the measure of copy. Something jarred him, and he didn't know what it was.

He pulled the "Dauphain" layout from his shoulder bag. Was it something about the layout? He set it up at the end of the cutting board and took a short hit of the beer. It was a good layout and it didn't need a map. He considered illustrators to do the final. It wasn't the layout, but something about it that bothered him. *Forget it, Salt, put business away.*

He rinsed and picked through two pounds of beans for tomorrow's meal and set them to soak in a deep bowl. The sausages were browned, the marinara went in with them, and he mixed it all together. He put on water for pasta and made a vinaigrette.

"Dad."

"Yo, Mike."

"Are these right?"

He looked at Mike's math homework. "Bring me some scratch paper and the book. I'll show you where the book is wrong."

Fractions. Once you had them in your head as graphic patterns of flow and balance you could do them, but most of the books still worked by rote. The smells got better as Charlie and Mike made patterns of numbers, how they worked, how they fit together, on the big cutting board. The smells couldn't hurt. Maybe all classrooms should have kitchens working in a corner. Mike understood his fractions now. Charlie was more pleased with that than with Dauphain.

The man in the Chevrolet, looking at the propped-up satellite and missile layout through 10 x 20 glasses, was very interested.

Thursday night. It was to be Yankee food.

Washington was a good place for food, but that, in itself, was a trap. Americans, naturally expansive, are generous hosts. Nothing but the best for our visitor. They thought of French food as an expensive treat, so they took Frenchmen to eat at Americanized French restaurants.

And so on, down the list of United Nations signatories. Ethiopians got Ethiopian food. Sort of.

It wouldn't do for Charlie: he was a culinary jingoist. To Charlie, there were no fish like the fish of home. He took his pride in Menemsha swordfish, Massachusetts Bay cod, Banks flounder, Sound sea trout. Also Maine lobster, Wareham cranberries, Maine russets, Acushnet pippins. When he traveled on assignment, he drank the wine of the country: salads of lush greens and California-crazy dressings in the Sonoma Valley; halibut and Dungeness crabs in Seattle; the misnamed but delightful Cincinnati chili in Cincinnati;

catfish and cole slaw in Huntsville, Alabama. Every place had its specialty, and he would find it. He was still working on Wheeling, but he was not yet discouraged.

So when Nikolai came, he would not serve him borscht but Yankee food.

His guests were almost due. Homework was going on upstairs and he was at his ease, or would have been without the little prickle of worry over something—his work, Corporal Wheeler, his rearranged office. Unrelated things. He unwrapped a wedge of Vermont cheddar and put out a bowl of California almonds on the table with an unruly plate of Triscuits, cheese transports that could compete with any damn cracker the Continent had to offer, bring 'em on, goddamnit. The air was sweet enough to walk on with the fragrance of baked beans. His cutting board was laid with produce and his rebeveled Henckels knives. Small cod filets, tomcod, lay waiting in dumb piscatorian sufferance by the range.

The Soviet delegation arrived first. Charlie threw open the door to him: "Nikolai! The bear appears! Wonderful to see you." They embraced like two wrestlers. There was a bond between the two they did not understand. It could have been Russian sadness at the core, disbelief in politics, disbelief in cities by country-born men. They didn't need the understanding, just the warmth.

Mike came down the stairs, sounding like a metal volleyball rolled down from the top. "Mike. Mike Salt," Nkolai said with his mischievous sideways look, "you are well this good evening?" Nikolai extended his hand.

Mike shook it manfully and said, "Hello. Glad to see you. Can I take your coat upstairs?"

"Yes. Absolutely. But first . . . " A quizzical eyebrow at Charlie. "Is okay?"

"Okay with you is okay with me, Nick."

He reached into his pocket and brought out a flat red package, small. "For my friend Mike."

Mike smiled. He liked the man and practiced talking like him, trying out throaty *k*'s and the formal phrases. "Thank you," he said, opening it while they watched. It was a medal with the profile of General Yuri Djanibekov.

"Is, in all USSR, great hero of cosmos. Leader of many missions to cosmos. Brave, intelligent researcher. Young people, your age, wish to grow in . . . " he looked at Charlie, ". . . his model? This is so?"

"Yessuh. Or example."

"Just so. A new hero instead of Buffalo Bill."

Mike looked at Charlie. "Who?"

"Tell you about him later, sport."

"And Sarah?" Nikolai asked.

Charlie walked to the phone and picked it up. "Sadie," he said, "will you come down here for a moment? Nikolai just arrived."

"Charlie," Nikolai asked, "how did you know she was on the phone?"

"Odds. She's sixteen. She's almost surely on the phone at any given time. It's as reliable as an intercom."

As Sarah came down the stairs, Charlie wished he had invested in ballet lessons. But she made it to the bottom. "Hello." The generous half-smile of a sixteen-year-old citizen of the real world being kind to folks from the constipated, shopworn world Charlie and his older friends lived in.

"For the young lady of estimable beauty, a small piece of beauty." He drew from the other pocket, by some practiced trick, a fresh, moist yellow rose. Sarah feigned a lack of surprise, but took the bloom immediately and gave back a smile worth a dozen ordinary roses. With a little awkwardness on her part, Nikolai captured her hand and kissed it. "The lady of the house is as good and as pretty as this house."

Again she did not speak, but smiled and, in camouflaged confusion, said, "Homework," and rushed up the stairs with her rose. Charlie could imagine the next phone call: "Ohmygod, please, a rose, how geeky. Do you, I mean, believe it? And kissing my hand, like, really. Like, we're in the movies from the fifties or something. Really, too queer." Impressed beyond belief, a celebrity for hours on the telephone network.

When the sound of Sarah's ascension had died away and Mike's haphazard trip up with Nikolai's coat was still shaking the hall light, Charlie said, "I'm telling Marina, writing her in Moscva tomorrow. 'Nick is too damn charming by half, kid. He is undoubtedly getting more ass over here than the French ambassador. Keep your hooks in him, Marina, or we'll have a sexual defection.'"

"Ah. Marina has her charms. In cold weather. Which we have some." Marina, his wife, was a civil engineer who had a good, sturdy body. She looked as if she had designed it herself. Charlie could see the advantages for Russian winter.

"You horny bastard, come on in here and have a drink."

"What are you making me drink now? Not some New England strange thing again. What? Cranberry juice and gin? Should have been vodka, besides. You got enough vodka?"

"Hell, yes, the front desk wonders what's in those red packages. Tonight, in honor of autumn, you get an old drink from New England. And when do I get to try some special Armenian Soviet drink?"

"Vodka. Like everywhere. Good for body and good for soul." He had a wonderful Armenian face, pear-shaped from a pale forehead to flaring jaws, sad eyes that, nevertheless, had wicked humor, large ears for listening well, a small nose lost on the big expanse between cheeks that burned red with laughter or excitement or pleasure.

Allen and Marjorie arrived as Charlie was getting down glasses. Marjorie pushed her three-hundred-watt smile in front of them and Allen slouched behind, hiding his light under a bushel.

Nikolai's charm swelled to the occasion. "Again I am seeing always too lovely women in this house. Hello to Marjorie and to Allen, also lovely but in different way. Hello to beautiful couple."

Marjorie gushed happily. Allen lifted up his bushel far enough to shake hands and show his bitter grin. "Proletarian night with Nikolai Tsiokolvsky. Are we eating New England folk food again?"

"Bugger off," Charlie said. "You'd be eating curds and whey if you weren't eating here."

"Mostly curds," Allen replied. Marjorie dug him in his too-apparent ribs. "Let's have a drink."

They were sitting at the big board watching Charlie work. "You're about to have an Acushnet Bullfrog."

"Oh, God. Another folk drink. I get too much of this at home," said Allen.

"You do not. We don't do enough folk work at home." Marjorie was a folklorist.

"You mean like planting rice and making bamboo flutes?"

"No, I mean cooking special and dressing up."

"I didn't know you liked dressing up," Charlie said. "Have you tried the nun and abbot outfits, yet?"

"Charlie . . ." Marjorie drew the syllables out through her smile and blush.

"Whatever's in the drink, put more in it," Allen said.

Nikolai beamed. "Sweet, but good. This is, once again?" Nikolai was trying to remember everything, it seemed, but

Charlie knew his memory was perfect. His bear act was a very comfortable and pleasant fraud. He was a powerful, graceful man beneath. Perhaps it was an artifact of his early assignments, who knew where. Presently, he was the cultural secretary of the Soviet Embassy.

"An Acushnet bullfrog. Three parts cold cider with one part dark rum, ice and an apple wedge."

"But a New England Yankee drink has in it rum? I am thinking rum comes from Caribbean places."

"Good rum in Cuba, I hear," Allen said.

"It is good. Someday you will taste it," Nikolai said with just as much friendly irony. "When your trade policy gets past—this is right?—adolescence?" The fencing was a feature of these evenings.

"Adolescence or senility. Rum's a part of New England sea tradition," Charlie said, "when we traded all over the Caribbean. We traded rum for slaves in the triple trade."

"Triple trade? Slaves?"

"Black serfs," Allen said.

The discussion was just long enough for Charlie to lightly poach the tomcod and broil it even more lightly with bread crumbs. The salads were done, and they had laid the table while they talked slavery and enlightenment. Sarah and Mike were called and Charlie presented while the food was hot, cutting short all philosophy. Schrod with lemon wedges, Boston baked beans, creamed cole slaw with blanched broccoli and carrots, cornbread baked with crumbled bacon, and two pitchers of Rolling Rock beer.

"In my country," everything paused at the beginning as Charlie took off his apron and sat down and Nikolai held up his hand, "is a man. I do not know what you will call him in this country, but he is important man. *Tamada*. *Tamada* is not host, not taking importance away from host, fine host." He gestured to Charlie. "But is making sure dinner and toasts and spirits go well, make harmony . . . is right? Yes, harmony. So. I will be *tamada* and make toast now. To this house, which is warm and welcomes us, and to this family. To our good and much-loved host. To beautiful ladies," his glass dipped to Marjorie and Sarah, "and to us together in understanding."

They drank.

"The schrod is getting cold," Allen observed. It was proletarian food, better than anything Leon d'Or served that night.

Mike and Sarah cleared the table and fed the dishwasher while Marjorie scooped ice cream onto hot Indian pudding.

"Why are not Yankees fat? This is my impression, yes? That they are thin people and say only a little." Nikolai drank sweet tea.

"Charlie's New England passport is about to expire." Allen poured another half-glass of beer.

"What is this against piano? This is page from magazine, yes?"

"What we call a layout. When I have problems with a page, I sometimes stick it up and let it speak to me. This one is bothering me. I didn't have time work on it today. It's still a little clumsy.

"*Perviy blin komom*. The first pancake is a lump." Nikolai could not resist a proverb.

"Is this for 'High Frontiers'?" Allen asked, and put it down on the cleared table between them. Allen was also an art director for Geographic. "Okay. These are missiles and decoys from the evil kingdom coming over the horizon. . . ."

"What is this?" asked Nikolai, pointing at the Dauphain missile cutaway.

"Are these little guys on the right infrared detection

satellites?" Allen continued. "Is that what these orange dashed lines are? Then a relay to what?"

"The DISCUS communication constellation."

"Okay, back to command central on the coast. This yellow communications line ought to be stronger, I think. Back to this green pulsing . . . green pulsing?"

"Blue-green laser. Communications to picket submarines."

"All this unnecessary expense of nations. Delicate balances, dangerous games for grown people to play with the world. Gorbachev has risked much so we do not play these games, anymore." Nikolai shook his head.

"And this?"

"A pop-up X-ray laser missile to disable the incoming missiles."

"Never coming in. This is talented, beautiful piece of machine pornography. Nothing more. All crazy. Our missiles, your missiles. And how would one missile do all of this? How could one missile shoot all of these . . ." he waved a derisive finger at the mythical Soviet invaders, "these making-believe, Ivan-the-Terrible, nightmarish stories?"

"I'm not the planner, Nikolai; I am the explainer. This is an X-ray laser missile."

"What powers this X-nightmare?"

"A small fission device."

"*Nuclear bomb*. Above us in cosmos? Madness."

"Most of your long-service satellites are powered by nuclear power plants," Allen said.

"Yes. Yes, true." Nikolai got up and walked heavily to the refrigerator. He was angry; not at Allen or at Charlie, but at the craziness in the cosmos. "Big difference between small power plant for research, observation . . . Yes, we o serve like you observe. This is healthy, I say, let us all observe more and more. . . . But this is not bomb." He poured a thumb-sized glass of vodka from the frozen bottle. "Not big damn bomb raining down products of fission on fields, children, friends, birds."

Nikolai drank down the tiny glass of vodka. "Also against treaty made between nuclear powers not to deploy such weapons. Craziness, Charlie."

"You may be right, Nikolai. I think you are right. But I'm going to explain the craziness the best way I can so that forty million people can look it in the eye."

"This is all handout stuff, the research?" Allen was looking at the "Dauphain" layout.

"Most of it. Some of it is cross pollination from other projects, other consultants. Some of it is just conjecture we can confirm."

"I hope so." Allen shook his head. "It could be touchy stuff."

"I think this should be published, Allen. Make clear to ordinary people what scientists are up to."

"I'll tell the Stone."

"Stone?"

"I'll tell the editor-in-chief that you approve, Nikolai. He's very influenced by Soviet opinion."

Nikolai sighed. "We should have let him go to Novosibirsk, this is true. He is still, after a year, displeased?"

"Until he goes to Novosibirsk."

Nikolai shook his head in sad acceptance of strange obsessions. Marjorie brought the pudding with ice cream and Mike brought the cookies. Sarah was on the phone.

Sleepers ride up and down, rising to dreams and sinking to deep cups of rest. Some—Charlie Salt was one—slept his dreams close to the surface of waking, and often, at the crests of his ride, woke.

Charlie woke in joint-still, eye-heavy perplexity, wondering what had disturbed him. Something in the pattern of his life or work still jarred. He watched the shapes of light on his ceiling. He rearranged them in his head. He rolled to the clock and it told him the time, 4:05, but nothing else. It was not enough. He folded the douve back with the flannel sheet. Anyone single without flannel sheets should have a clean dog, he thought. He rose and put on his big white robe.

The stairs were long and profound and down. He was still loose and deep. He stood in his kitchen hardly knowing how he got there and didn't even want juice. The pale rectangle at the end of the big cutting board was the "Dauphain" layout. It, with other small disparate things, troubled him. His feet were cool on the clean, cold floor. In that state of suspension from life and will, he was too open, too vulnerable to reach for the door and swing it shut against the images approaching.

He saw her solemn, sweet face coming in the front door before him. Saw that he was a little high. They had been to a party. He had sung Irish songs and sea songs and, coming home, lullabies he hadn't sung for years, since Sarah and Mike were little. He heard her voice, heard her say: "The butcher block is too new. We had a rule about that." She wasn't any more provocative than that. She knew him too well, played him without words the way a fly fisherman will play a trout with a barbless hook and the lightest leader. Did she need more words? Never.

He knew he should reach out and close the door, but he was too open, still too sleepy. *Close the door. I can't.*

He kissed her. She had a small mouth, incredibly sweet, rich, a trace of wine still with her tongue. She played him with her tongue, the lightest of leaders. He pulled her to him, needing her, combing his fingers into her fine hair and taking

it in his grasp, pulling her mouth into him. Her breathing
was faster. He pulled her whole body into him. She reached
toward him with her body. He needed everything, but her
mouth was so rich, he needed one thing most. She lifted
easily, protesting playfully, pushing him ineffectively away
while drawing him powerfully to her. He could smell her
fragrance. Her dress was smooth; he threw it back. Not as
smooth as her thighs, or the catch of her topography, where
her buttocks bloomed back from her legs.

My God, he loved her ass.

He was impatient with her panties. Extravagant panties,
tiny on her, almost ceremonial, he dropped them behind
him.

Charlie, the dreamer with his feet cold on the floor, stood
large and stiff under the big robe, almost seeing the panties
near his cold feet, watching his own head buried between
her legs, tasting her, smelling her, feeling her wonderful firm
and soft ass in both grasping palms and she could not play
him now at all, which was what she wanted, to lose the
control. She could only surge into his mouth and, pleading,
push his hands down so that his fingers found her depths
smooth and wet. She could only surge with his mouth and
rhythmic tongue and his fingers moving in her, and he knew
who held the rod now, as she surged and caught and the
muscles under her tummy and scar and crotch and ass
tightened in her own inward rush of escape.

He tore at his belt, she plucked at his zipper. He let his
pants drop and pulled her down with his hands grasping the
softness of her ass again, down around him, but he made
noise. Cattle frightened, pigs rooting, dogs dreaming of
rabbits running, bears huffing as he pushed smoothly into
her, wet, rich. Opening his eyes, he saw her eyes open and
staring at him wide, almost frightened, saw her small mouth

open without sound, heard his own rutting noises and then he came into her as she came again, pulling her gratefully, gently into him, confused and dizzy against the big board baptized.

His feet were cool on the floor. He saw it all, surged at his own grasp through the open robe until the room swam. He hated the open door but couldn't deny it. He almost fell when it came to him. He couldn't hate the door because he couldn't hate her. He leaned over the board, four years worn, with his breath fast and heart drumming. He was twisted between longing and anger, sleepy, spent, confused. *Charlie Salt*, he said through the drumming in his chest, *you had it all once, and when—if ever—will it come again? Maybe never. Maybe.*

He sat down in the living-room rocker. Clear, awake, a little dizzy. In the preternatural sight that sometimes comes after sex of any kind he looked aimlessly through his window and saw the pattern coalesce with frightening speed. He saw a Chevrolet, green or blue in the streetlight, and knew he had been seeing it for days. He saw the figure of Corporal Wheeler, the rummaged, straightened offices. Murray searching for new leads in sensitive places, Pentagon back alleys. He saw the two times, before, when they had put together too much off-the-shelf information and caught heat from classified, even secret sources. Dauphain? Why Dauphain, what was secret about a plan?

There was a man in the Chevrolet. Charlie saw him drinking from a white cup of coffee, tea, chocolate, who the hell cared? Why is a man sitting outside my house at four in the goddamned morning?

He was angry. He was frightened. He wanted to live on his elm-arched street with his children and without crazy men in Chevrolets killing Corporal Wheeler.

He sat rigidly in the rocking chair, in the shadows where the man in the Chevrolet could not see him. To Charlie, he seemed supernaturally large and foreboding. The man got out of the car and walked away. He returned with another white cup. *Go away*, Charlie Salt asked him.

At 4:45, as the tree branches began to be visible against the sky, he did go away, starting the engine and moving very slowly down the street.

He could get up then. He poured himself a glass of orange juice and drank it as if it were Tusker. *Are you crazy, Charlie? You must be crazy. There is nothing to this. You're a paranoid, you're romanticizing this whole thing. You're puffing up plots against a nobody art director. Cool it. When's the last time you were the object of a big, secret Star Wars plot? Chill out, Charlie! You have been up too long. Breathe into a paper bag or something. Woof, you are losing it, boy.*

He made lunches, a treat for the guys. They came down, unimpressed that he was already up. They had given up commenting on his eccentricities around third grade. They were raucous and noisy and reassuring at breakfast. Homework was done. He knew he was crazy.

But he took a different route to a different Metro stop, staying with crowds. *So I get to be crazy. I'm an art director.*

Murray Hofnung didn't show up for work.

Chapter 5

"INSPECTOR CARLTON DEAUVILLE, PLEASE." Charlie stood fidgeting at his drafting table, fooling with a mechanical pencil and watching clouds scud behind rooftop satellite dishes, so he was almost startled when Deauville's voice came on the line.

"'Lo. Deauville, here. What you got?"

"Inspector Deauville, this is Charlie Salt over at the *Geographic*. I've got a . . . problem, something that doesn't make sense."

Deauville replied very simply, "Not the chaplain."

Charlie heard the toothpick in his mouth making the words lengthen and drawl even more. He tried to break through Deauville's nonchalance. "Corporal Wheeler's death. I think it may have something to do with me."

"Tell me." The nonchalance was impregnable.

"The night he died . . . the night he was killed, I think, someone looked through my files and Printing and Engraving's drawers. I think I know what they were looking for."

There was a pause for toothpick chewing before the slow bass voice said, "Go ahead."

"Sometimes we've put some stuff together in a layout, a page dummy, that is sensitive material. We've guessed too

close to secret material before. Did you see our piece on the
Stealth bomber?"

No reply. Charlie figured that as a negative.

"Same thing, sensitive stuff. This time . . . someone came
and looked all through my office but didn't find the layout
or the sketches to take with them. They wanted to know
what we had. They don't want it published. I don't know
why. Corporate Wheeler was killed. Last night, I saw a car
outside my house with a man in it. I think I've seen the car
before, and I know I saw it again today.

"This morning Murray Hofnung, the researcher who put
together a lot of the information in the package, didn't come
to work. I can't get him on the telephone." Charlie stopped.
He felt foolish.

There was a long pause, with no sound from Deauville.

"Murray always comes in," Charlie continued. "I don't
live on a busy street. I'm not making this up. I've got two
kids, and I'm worried. Are you listening to me?"

After a beat, indifferent, "This Hilyard Hofnung . . . "
Deauville's voice was from the South, thick and slow like a
warm caramel.

"Murray Hofnung."

"How long he's been 'missing'?"

"Nine and a half hours."

"He drink?"

"Not like that."

"He gay?"

'I never asked him or any of his girlfriends. Goddammit,
what's that go to do with it?"

"One day's not missing. Family problems, distant relative
dies, going on a toot—even an occasional toot—sick in bed,
broke his leg last night walking home. He's not missing yet.
You'll get word."

"Sergeant . . . "

"Inspector. Inspector Carlton Deauville, Homicide."

"Look, Deauville, I'm worried about two kids and some fucking maniac outside my house. My house, my kids. I know Murray. I know my office. I know what I do, and someone's got their hand in it."

Another leisurely chewing pause. "Mr. Salt? Will you give me your home address and phone number, please?" Charlie gave it to him, and he took it down. "Mr. Salt, this is all interesting, and I'm sure you're worried. But you have very little of a substantive nature here for reporting a crime. You don't know what the crime is and I've got a crime here that at least I know. You understand? I can't help you. No way."

"My kids have to be protected, Inspector. Are you hearing me? Do you have kids?"

Deauville shifted the toothpick from one side of his mouth to the other. He spoke again. "I can't act on this information you've given me, because it doesn't come together. Government doesn't kill night guards. Government doesn't stake out art directors. Unless you're getting your information the wrong way. You doing that, Mr. Salt?"

Charlie was wearied by anxiety. "That's not our style."

"You and Mr. Hofnung? That's not your style?"

"The magazine's style."

"Mr. Salt, take down these numbers, where you can reach me all the time." Charlie copied two numbers with different exchanges. "I'm not saying you're crazy, not saying you don't see good. I'm telling you that things in all likelihood of probability are going to turn out fine and you'll feel better. If something else turns up, any time, you call me and we'll talk again. Right now you should go home to your two kids and have supper and cease off worrying about this. I have to go myself."

Carlton Deauville walked down the hall, crowded with file cartons, trying to dismiss Charlie Salt's worries. He concentrated on the scenario that made the most sense, the least complicated one. But he hated chance.

"Mr. Salt," the maître d' at the Jefferson greeted him. "Citizen Tsiokolvsky and friend are in your usual booth near the fire."

"Thank you, Stanos." The sixtyish maître d' was an emigre Czech and managed to look something other than bored in his tuxedo. "It's time for fires again. Will you please have one of the guys bring me a double Bushmills with soda and a twist?" Stanos nodded.

"Nikolai."

The bear stood and hugged him, then held him at arm's length, looking at him sideways, trying to jolly away the depleted half-smile Charlie wore. "You having a bad day? Enough. Day is over. Now we are having a good day, okay? A little drink, a little talk. Meet my good friend Petrov Kruskin, a real Russian born in Moscva." Kruskin rose and greeted Charlie with a handshake hard enough to feel like a test. Charlie passed, but just.

"He is engineer come for seminar at MIT in Cambridge, Massachusetts. Good for him, I say, but should come to see his old friend and practice the language. Say something about engineering, Petrov." Nikolai sat Charlie on a chair and slapped Petrov with bearish strength on the back.

Now Petrov gave him a smile, as friendly a smile as stainless steel bridgework could permit. "Glad to be here. Good city, I like it." His English didn't need practice, and he seemed pleasant.

"Hey," Nikolai said with apology in his voice, "I promise Petrov something of you. Not inconvenient if you can't do it, but, look, I told him, who is athlete, not like me," Nikolai patted his paunch with a satisfied smile, "that you would take him on some runs. Show him good runs in Washington, okay?"

"Sure. Glad to, Petrov. Tomorrow be too early? After work?"

"Tomorrow would be perfect. I would enjoy this a lot. Where?"

"What do you want to run? Two miles, four?"

"I will run what you run."

"Good. A slow three, slow enough for you to practice your English, which is pretty good right now, by the way."

"Many thanks."

The way Petrov Kruskin looked at him, Charlie suspected it would be a hard three miles. Kruskin was a competitor, a pusher. *Good,* thought Charlie as his drink came, *I can use the push.*

"But you had a bad day?" Nikolai asked.

"Strange. Yessuh, bad enough. You know the layout I showed you?"

"Technological pornography." He put up his palms to show his belief in its obscenity.

Charlie put down his drink and rubbed one hand down over his face and beard in a habitual gesture of worry and thought. "You know, Nick, I think someone's after me about it. I am probably crazy as the proverbial shithouse rat . . . "

Kruskin looked closely at Nikolai, who replied in Russian, softly, then said to Charlie, "Told him it was rural American colloquial expression. He likes it. Go ahead, Charlie. This is not good, right?"

"Well, I am probably crazy, but I think I've stepped on some intelligence toes by putting together some of the wrong

. . . or right . . . stuff. I probably shouldn't have showed it to you, you know, but I didn't expect any trouble. I think there's a guy watching my house, and I sometimes imagine that a guard at the *Geographic* may have been killed by someone looking through my office for the layout and file."

Charlie laughed suddenly and not very mirthfully. "Okay, I've told someone. They'll ship me away . . ." he winked at Kruskin, ". . . to the gulag for psychiatric retreading."

Kruskin, ignoring the wink, said to Nikolai, "You told me this was not a nation of gangsters."

"It is not. He's crazy." He turned to Charlie. "You're crazy, you know that, little brother? Crazy as outhouse rat, for sure. You know what I think now?"

Without waiting for an answer, he went on. "I think it is important for *National Geographic* to publish this X-ray thing. Respected magazine, shows a climate of distrust unhealthy for both sides in era of glasnost. Important you should tell Stone, 'Publish it.' Show everybody. Yes."

"But you are worried. I see it. You are worried about being in danger? Worse about Mike and Sarah being in danger. Never. Not in this country, not in mine. Maybe in Libya or in Columbia, but not here. Truly. Trust me: I am expert on American culture." He beamed, and Charlie could almost believe him.

"We can run," Kruskin said with real kindness, "to get your mind away from it. Okay. Tomorrow afternoon after work."

"Good. I can meet you at the towpath, or pick you up at the Tunlaw Gate, or . . ."

"Nikolai has told me your address. I hope you do not mind. I will drive to your house at, what, seven?"

"Better six-thirty. I have to make dinner for the guys. You can join us if you want."

"Let us see how tired you make me, friend Charlie."
Kruskin smiled in steely assurance, and Nikolai beamed at
both of them.

∇

Chapter 6

"You want me to bring down a flashlight, Dad?"

"Hmm?" Charlie looked up at Sarah from *The Vegetarian Epicure*. It was a snotty, snobbish book by vicious anti-carnivores, but good cooking. "Flashlight?"

"Ohmygod. You are so spacy sometimes. A flashlight. You've got every other light in the house on. Can I turn off some? How about the one in the basement toilet?"

"Yeah, kid, turn that off, will you? I don't know, early nights now. I kind of miss long summer evenings. I'm compensating."

"You and the electric company. I mean, really. What is all this? We'll get sunburn."

"Cheers me up. Indulge me."

Mike came in. "What's for dinner, Dad? Why all the lights?"

"Potato and corn chowder with cornbread. The lights are to dispel the dark gloom of approaching winter."

"Veggies," Mike said, looking at the cookbook over Charlie's arm, "Are we going to start eating fruits and nuts and berries again?"

"Indulge him," Sarah said caustically. "He's getting old."

Mike nodded and pronounced the diagnosis: "Old-timer's disease."

It was a white frame house with a big garden, a block off Military Road in Arlington. It fronted a lane drifted with oak leaves and backed onto woods, a sweet little house not too recently painted and not so fastidiously kept that it attracted attention. It was an easy street to park on, day or night, and a few extra cars—the blue Chevrolet and Larry's Datsun Z among them—blended unobtrusively.

Inside on a round oak table spread with the *Washington Times*, Wilson, who managed the safe house for the Outfit, was carving a jack-o-lantern with a Gerber Mark II survival knife.

"You're going to stab yourself," the man from the Chevrolet said.

"No, it works good. It's sharp as hell, and it's thin enough to make these turns, see?"

"Make the eyes bigger. They look piggy, like Bill's old Ops man. What was his name?"

"Him. That sonofabitch. I'll make him the jack-o-lantern, but it'll look smarter than him."

"Probably be smarter, too."

Larry came in with Nadine Wilson. They put down a pot of coffee and cups and a plate of brownies. Larry was chewing one already. "Good brownies, you guys." He looked at his watch. "Almost time."

The doorbell rang, and Nadine went to answer it. She brought back a young Hispanic in slacks and sweater, and a black about the same age in Levis, a turtleneck, and a blazer. They introduced themselves and sat down.

"Guillermo." The Hispanic held up his hand and looked around to the others.

"Peter," the black man said, and nodded in no special direction.

"Good brownies," Larry said, still chewing as he offered the plate. Wilson kept at the jack-o-lantern and the man from the Chevrolet watched Guillermo and Peter with his hands folded on the table, as if he could determine why he was growing old by looking at the young men taking his place.

The phone rang. Wilson held up the fighting dagger and his pumpkin-sticky hands to Nadine, who smiled and answered it. "Hello . . . Yes, and the two new members, Guillermo and Peter . . . Very well . . ."

She put a speakerphone on the table, careful not to get it near the seeds and pulp. She pressed its button and said, "You there, Bill?"

The speaker came to life. "Talk to me, people."

"Larry here. Our Dauphain situation is complicated but stable. We should have some direction on where to go from here, Bill."

"Let's see where we've been and go from there. How much do you think Salt knows?"

"The first contact was last week. Salt's rough sketch had a measured drawing of the Dauphain bird, correct in all details for surface configuration and for general cross section inside. FMS interconnecting communications links, the whole deal. We don't know how he got so much information. He's got no clearance. We know he's thick with the Russians. He's got to be a Soviet operative of some stripe, has to be to hang with Tsiokolsvky."

"Why don't we have the layout and the sketches?"

"As soon as we learned what direction he was taking with it, our night team went into Salt's office at the *Geographic*. Here we had a misadventure."

The man from the Chevrolet watched the faces of Guillermo and Peter for any change. Nothing.

"We built a good accidental robbery mayhem structure around that, Bill. There's no problem, there. But the layout was not in evidence."

"What about the burglars we terminated?"

"Unavoidable, couldn't be helped. Once again, we built a tight structure of street violence around it."

"Containment, gentlemen. It's getting more and more difficult to keep this localized. Where is the layout, and what are we doing about containment?"

The man from the Chevrolet spoke up. "He carries it with him from his office to his home. He puts it up and looks at it."

"Who is that?"

"Burns, Bill. Steve Burns from payments section. They pulled me off to do some street work again."

"Burns, you were with me in Korea in 'sixty-four, right? Good man. Now, why don't we have the layout?"

"Keeps it close, Bill. We can get it, but it's more wetwork. I don't favor a burglary scenario. There are two children; that attracts the press and makes cops that much more thorough. I favor a car accident, a street mugging, or a thorough opera setup. Unfortunately, we've taken Hofnung off the roster with an opera setup, so that's closed to us."

"Which opera?"

"*Madame Butterfly*. They'll find two bodies, Hofnung and a gay hooker in his apartment with some bad cocaine. They'll turn him up in two or three days, depending on the air-conditioning system in his apartment house and chance visitors."

"Salt?"

"I say leave him tonight. Last report, he had every light in the house on. He suspects something. Let's give him a night to lose some caution and run our stageplay tomorrow after-

noon. Crime in the streets, mugging and unfortunate death.
After Salt is gone, we'll get the layout. Done."

"Larry?"

"Sounds good to me, Bill."

"You guys need Burns. Got some experience in the field.
Solid sense, good moves. Good. So the night team will watch
tonight, get some relief in the morning, and take over again
in the afternoon for the theatrics. Containment. Any questions?"

"That should do it, Bill," Larry said.

"Bill?"

"That you, Burns?"

"Yeah. This Salt, he's a flako. He's unpredictable. I read
him as a wild card. He'll be a problem."

"Not to you guys. Good luck." The speakerphone commenced an annoying dial tone, and Wilson pushed its
button with the point of his knife.

Burns rose and went into the kitchen for another cup of
coffee. He put down the pot and lifted his cup, staring past
it to the woods behind the house. Solid sense. Good moves.
He allowed himself a pale smile and an extra crinkle around
his eyes. He was a field man again.

$\triangledown$

Chapter 7

Bob balisterio stood with his feet spread, hands in hip pockets, pugnaciously confronting the broad, downlit wall. Cliprails held empty layout sheets, and the light table to his right glowed with the colored jewels of seventy Kodachrome slides.

When Charlie walked in, Bob was almost ready, dithering nervously on the edge of some major swoop of action. Charlie could almost smell the heat of Bob's concentration and read the expression of a man impatient for his muse to arrive. Balisterio, the Sicilian layout hit man. Charlie loved passion.

"Bite him, Hiram, He bit ya fatha."

Bob turned to him, slightly annoyed and puzzled. "What?"

"I don't know what it means, either, but my father-in-law used to throw it in at odd times. A New England phrase, roughly translatable as 'Go for it!' You about to kick ass with 'Star Wars'.

"Yeah. Talk to me. Chew the fat here with me. Get this bastard going."

Bob turned to a table with a paper cutter and a waxer. He dealt out a stack of fifty four-by-five black-and-white prints selected from the Kodachrome slides. Of the two thousand frames Jillian Ansara had shot for the story, these were the

selects. They had begun as ideas. Preresearch had put together a rough package of background information on the
subject and had suggested two dozen consultant on specific
specialties. The writer of the article, freelancer John Boslough, had met with the science editor, Tom Canby, and the
picture editor, Gabriel Cooper, and Jillian and Charlie. Some
of the broad strokes of the story were always worked out
before the story session with the editor-in-chief, the director
of photography, and the associate editors. But it was Stone's
magazine, and his sense that would guide the story at the
beginning and again at the end. In between, the field men
took over.

The writer and the photographer beat the bushes, appear-
ing at every weapons design installation, every contractor,
every grantee researching satellite deterrence, every conference. They traveled the country and both oceans, separately
and together. They called into the *Geographic*—updating
their plane and hotel reservations through the travel office,
asking for a Toyota Celica at the SeaTac Airport on the
twelfth and transfer me to Gabe Cooper, will you?

They talked to the Mother Church from the field, standing up at booths or lying down on motel beds. Either one of
them could punch the *Geographic* phone-card number in
the dark, left-handed.

Boslough reported to the science editor. "I saw Frank
D'Alestrino, today. He has some ideas about chemical lasers
that make NASA nervous." He took notes, typed fragments,
made outlines, talked and talked and talked. His ideas for
possible photos were respectfully, gingerly laid before the
picture editor, Gabe Cooper, ramrod of the story, who dis-
cussed them with the director of photography, Tom Kennedy. Jillian's film arrives in bunches. The yellow boxes of
processed slides passed through pre-editing, where consis-

tent flaws of focus or lighting or color were considered and reported as possible breakdowns in the photographer's equipment. The important thing—the only thing—was getting the picture at the right time and the right place.

The Stone had been a shooter. He still was, still photographed the stories he liked in Southeast Asia, Tibet, Central America. His whole dictum on technical photography was summed up in the single, dry sentence he used to meet alibis of all kinds: "F-8, and be there."

Gabe Cooper ran the yellow boxes through his slide viewer, a straightforward piece of equipment designed by Stone himself. He sat alone in his dimmed room and stabbed the advance button at the pace of a slow heart, that occasionally fibrillated. He looked through Jillian's eyes as she discovered the subject through her lens, nodding his head occasionally, leaning forward to pull a single frame out for the small select pile beside the viewer. The subjects changed, the images were sometime repetitious as she bracketed her shots for the right exposure, the best, the most dramatic angle. Come on, Cooper said to her eyes, shoot it simple, give me the story. But Jillian kept reaching, and then there was a shot that made him glad she had reached so hard. He nodded his head and added it to the little pile. He kept punching the advance.

There were words, pictures, and then Charlie made the third horse in the troika. What couldn't be photographed, what couldn't be said, what gathered up and condensed and focused information was Charlie's contribution. Charlie worked out of thin air; he created what couldn't be captured. He worked with Tom Canby and with Gabe Cooper to complete the story, often to build the piece on which the story pivoted, the central illustration that freed the writer from paragraphs of explanation and allowed the photogra-

pher to concentrate on people and action. In "Star Wars,"
Charlie had three pieces: an explanation of a chemical laser,
a flyby of satellites hardened against lasers, and Dauphain.

Balisterio and Charlie sat and shuffled the prints.

"Jesus, Bob, this is such a damn good photo. Jillian is
good."

"Yeah, but it's the third vertical shot we'd have of a
machine with a face under it. Good shot, but it don't fit."

"This big, bleak landscape of the desert around Lawrence
Livermore Lab is aces, but how are we going to use it?"

"Could use it behind the whole lead spread, so . . ." And
Balisterio sketched a layout on a pad of quarter-sized page
layouts.

"Nice lead spread for a story on Lawrence Livermore, but
it doesn't say Star Wars."

"Mmm." Balisterio nodded. "Let's get Gabe down here."

"This damn story bugs me, Bob."

"Why? If you got through 'Sleep,' you can get through
anything. Hell, I don't agree with the story or the principle,
but He Who Must Be Obeyed says we do a Star Wars story,
we do a Star Wars story."

Charlie decided not to tell Balisterio his fears for now. He
busied himself with sketching a new layout for the lead
spread, composing with his thick-lead pencil and letting his
stomach unflutter. Murray was off with some honey,
shacked up for the day playing hide the sausage. Murray had
the face of a ten-year-old who had just found a peephole into
the girls' shower room, a brash and likable face always about
to erupt into a pun. Murray was unharmed. No one would
hurt him; no one could. He was too well-intentioned. There
was no conspiracy. *Do I hear voices yet? This is either the
onset of schizophrenia or Old-timer's. Plots, watchers in the
night. You've seen too many movies, sport.*

Gabe Cooper sloped in and folded his bony length into a chair facing the wall. " 'Ey. What the hell are you up to, Charlie?"

"The best I can, Gabe. I'm thinking of a lead spread that segues into something like this, a gatefold spread about orbital mechanics."

Charlie had divided the three-page spread into horizontal bands that began to ripple as they moved right. Each band explained a principle of orbital mechanics, how a satellite's movements are governed by speed and the height of its orbit, how any threat to a satellite was governed by the same principles.

"Damn," Gabe said, holding the little layout and listening to Charlie explain. "We need this sonofabitch; the cocky sonofabitch is right."

"It shouldn't be the turn, though." Charlie was protecting the pagespread after the lead. He slipped his drawing under the grip rail over the third blank spread Bob had laid out. "The lead wants to be cold and mysterious and threatening. That's the story, isn't it?" Gabe nodded, and Bob shuffled the prints. "I was thinking of that NASA picture from the shuttle, the unfolding communications satellite, cropped to the left like . . . this. Add black image on this side and drop the title out in red, here, with dropout copy, an introduction by the editor to the subject."

Charlie was drawing on a small layout sheet; Balisterio was drawing his own version. "And Jillian's dusk shot of the B-52 with the laser turret on the turn, then."

"Fuck her if she can't take a joke," Charlie said.

"Sooner that than take away my lead and give it to some fighter-jock astronaut who doesn't know a camera from an airsick bag." Jillian Ansara was leaning against the doorframe. Her arms were folded, and her large, brown, experienced eyes were fixed on the back of Charlie's head.

Charlie looked back and saw that her eyes had him skewered. *That's what the pain in my head was,* he said to himself. He didn't stop drawing against the wall but held his foot back behind him. "Here, Gabe, untie my shoe, will you?"

"How's that, Mr. Salt?" He was smiling at the skeweree.

"So my foot will fit more comfortable in my mouth, Mr. Cooper. Perhaps you will tell Ms. Ansara that I'm afflicted by a genetic difficulty that makes me say wicked things. Completely beyond my control. Support mental health. More to be pitied than censured. Brother, can you spare a dime." He kept drawing the full-size version of the orbital mechanics piece. "Do you thing she'll hurt me, Mr. Cooper? Does she go about armed?"

"Last guy who took away her lead . . . What was that jamoca's name, Bob? Didn't find enough of him for dental identification. Little bitty pieces. And they were singed."

"Why the NASA lead?" she asked, unmoving. She was a woman of medium height with good shoulders, strong fore-arms, and powerful hands that looked as if they could hold a Nikon through a typhoon. Her face had the cheekbones and copper-alloy glow that her Navajo grandmother had passed on to her. She was lean but shapely, a remarkably attractive woman to men who didn't find her mannish. Charlie didn't. Charlie was shy around attractive women. He expressed his shyness in an unfortunate brashness that could be grating.

"It's more sinister, colder, more spacelike. Of course, it's up to Bob," Charlie said to her without looking back, "but for my money, this shuttle-photo lead is archival, something we can't reproduce without our own space shuttle and launch facility. This is a look at the orbital environment and not a well-lighted shot of mechanized garbage cans hoping to go into orbit. Maybe the garbage can colors are great. Maybe you took it at the right time of day. But it ain't the real stuff."

Bob cleared his throat as Jillian said, "Jesus."

Bob stepped into the building tension. "Charlie's onto something, Jills, even if he hammers it home a little hard. Plus, I wouldn't want to drop type out of any Jillian Ansara shot. We start with the orbital shot and move on to your killer laser on the turn, then to a spread of orbital mechanics."

"How many images are we going to lose to ABC's, Gabe?"

"We've got plenty of room, Jillian. You've done a hell of a good job on this story . . ." But she was gone. Gabe stood and grabbed Charlie around the neck with his elbow, rubbing his bald pate with his knuckles in gentle censure. "Charlie, Charlie, you charmer you. Can you manage to say something reassuring to the next woman you talk to? Something about her weight problem or her complexion, maybe? I've got to go unruffle the Queen Shooter. *Adios.*

When he was gone, Charlie turned with the layout blocked out in tones of black and white thick pencil. "I can work most of these in gray so that . . .," he began, but Bob was sitting in his chair with his fingers laced over his sternum, looking at Charlie intently and shaking his head. "You got the brain of a flea, Charlie."

"Hey. What did I do? I was right. She's got some hair across her ass, that's no fault of mine, Don Balisterio."

"Dufus. You know, if that were some young cartographer or one of the picture editors or almost anyone other than a good looking woman, you'd be the soul of kindness and tact. Charlie, you're one of the sweetest men I know and yet you get harsh with women over and over. What is it with you? You going gay on me, sweetums? Or are you just going to wait until old age sets in and date someone from the old folks' home? You worry me, you big tuna fish."

Charlie sat in his office staring out the window, eating a fresh chicken salad on pumpernickel, leaning against a door that kept swinging open with Kim behind it. Her face, her small mouth, her full cheeks advertising freckles, her perfect ears. "Charlie." The way she said it and let it carry most of what she had to say. He chewed and didn't taste and was angry, as he sometimes was because she had said too little. When he tried to remember his life with her, those meaningful tones faded faster than anything else, and he was left with too few words to tack down moments and the times they had spent together. He chewed faster and leaned harder against the door, hoping it would stay closed.

A knock on his office door. "Come," he called, but he didn't turn away from the window until the door shut behind someone.

"Look," Jillian began, "Gabe told me to come by. He said you were right about the . . ."

She stopped, looking at Charlie chewing and staring at her. She had never seen a look like his, a look as full of many thoughts, as sad as a dog in the pound, and as weary. Was it possible he was on the edge of tears?

"Well, you're busy, and I . . ."

Charlie put down his sandwich and rose. He motioned for Jillian to follow him. He stood at his drafting table and laid down a card stock layout sheet. He took a broad chisel-point felt tip and ran his hands over the sheet as if he were feeling for lines of direction in it. Then he began, slowly, to form letters. They were letters as graceful as he himself wanted to be, assured curves and firm straights. His hand and arm and body and breathing were behind the chisel point and the letters appeared like spirits called up by spells his body was casting.

The sheet said "Sorry" in large letters, then he shifted to a smaller nib and to a smaller, more flowing style, "is the offering of an erring friend, a balm for bruised feelings." At the end, he dropped the descender of the G low and picked it up into a fanciful scroll of three lobes and many passes, all stroked slowly, hypnotically to Jillian. He put away the pens and handed the layout to Jillian. He looked down at the carpet, out the window, didn't trust himself to say anything, and looked up at her with a frown that a less astute observer might have thought angry. But Jillian Ansara was the Queen Shooter; she knew people better than that. She could read some of the pain in his eyes. She was an explorer, and wondered about what she couldn't read. She wanted to say something but he spoke first. "Good shoot. It's more than hardware. Nice stuff."

She nodded. "Thanks." Another silence, and she looked at the piece of calligraphy. "They tell me you can cook, too."

He snorted softly in self-amusement and nodded. "Little bit. Shepherd food, fry it till it gives up."

"You know how I make ham and eggs?" she asked. He shook his head. "First I say, Waiter?'"

He smiled and nodded. His face went somber again, then it relaxed. "Do you like fish?"

"Anything that swims."

"Allen Carroll is coming by with Marjorie Thursday night at seven. You could join us. Would you like to bring someone?"

"No,"she said, and looked him plainly in the eye.

As she walked down the hall carrying her lettered apology, she wondered how she came to rethink Charlie so quickly. Why had she invited herself to his home? Had she been too bold? This was not a question the Queen Shooter asked herself too often. And why be bold with a man she had never thought of? He was a strange man. Just before she got to

Gabe's office and put it out of her mind, she realized that
she had probably thought about Charlie Salt before he stuck
his thick-lead pencil into her story.

Charlie sat down with a clump and a squeal from Edward
Everett Crocker's spare chair. Ned Crocker turned from his
work and beamed, an engaging, courtly expression full of
curiosity and enthusiasm with a soupçon of delightful lar-
ceny. Ned had, over forty-five years, wriggled and swum and
bounded through the world for the Geographic. He'd been
to coronations at the court of St. James, circumcisions in
painted mud huts, feasts of stuffed camel, and teas with the
Dalai Lama. He had dived with Captain Cousteau and had
taken the first color photos underwater. (The chair's squeal
came to him by way of his right ear; hearing in the left had
been compromised by an incident during decompression in
the Red Sea.) At seventy-two, his gait was, properly, a sailor's
rolling stride that still covered ground. Every writer and
photographer for as long as the Society survived would be
measured against his inimitable standard.

"My dear friend," he said with the broad vowels of his
Boston childhood, "how delighted I am to see you." The
magic of the man was that, Captain Cousteau and the Dalai
Lama notwithstanding, he was genuinely delighted to see
you. Between Charlie and Ned, moreover, there was the
special bond of explainers, storytellers. Charlie went to Ned
as his touchstone, to rub suspect metal against him and read
its worth. He went to him as the repository of wisdom,
knowledge, scatology, and professional gossip.

"Ned," Charlie began, "I've reported you to the National
Organization for Women for that scandalously misogynous
story you told me last week."

"You didn't tell them where I was, did you?" Don't do

that. They'll put two and two together, and before you know it I'll be up against the wall with a last cigarette." He threw his hands up piteously.

"Question."

"Yes, my boy."

"Did you ever run into a situation where a story . . ." Charlie chose his words carefully, "impinged on an intelligence operation?"

"Yes." The answer was immediate. "During the War, of course, this happened often. Intelligence networks were large and pervasive throughout South America, and there were several instances of just such conflicts."

"And after the war? Were there other times when the goals were less distinct than Hitler and fascism against democracy and FDR?"

Ned laughed a single, bitter note. "Not the balanced opposites I expect of you, Charles."

Charlie raised his hands, palms to, and shrugged with his eyes closed. Okay, a sloppy pairing.

"Again, yes," Ned went on, "In South America and, shockingly, here in this country. Some conflicts of what were usually referred to as 'national security' but were more often matters of prevailing prejudice. Now, I am not without my own prejudices, as you know, Charles, but I fight against them. Certain intelligence figures from one agency and another came to me and asked me to veer in my coverage or, worse, to provide information to them."

"What did you do?"

"That was a long time ago. Let me ask you about your situation. What are you going to do? Perhaps we can learn from my errors."

"I seem to have unwittingly stumbled onto something the Pentagon doesn't want known."

Ned shook his head and made a concerned sound in his throat, then brightened. "I like you, Charles. Always have. You never do anything cheaply, always on a large scale. I like it, it has Size," he said, using a phrase that had become a comic trademark.

"My question is this, oh guru: What the fuck should I do?"

Ned shook his head slowly as if refusing an applicant for a mortician's position, "How can I tell you what to do, my boy? I can only tell you what I think may be right for a journalist in the situation."

"Ned, we come out once a month. That doesn't excuse us. In the old days—you should forgive the expression—a lot of what we did wasn't journalism, a lot of the writers and shooters were traveling PR men. The stuff you did was journalism, Ned, it explained the world. Now, with Stone, the magazine and all of us with it are confronting real problems. We don't have to see Ethiopia as costumes and best efforts by government officials. We see a famine as death. I'm not a decorator, I'm a journalist. You always have been. Tell me, Ned."

"Then, like a journalist, I must ask more questions. The story you're writing . . ."

"Star Wars."

"Oh, why do we do stories like that? It isn't our meat, you know. Be that as it may, you are using a piece of information or technology that displeases . . . certain people . . . powerful people. What is it? May I know?"

"As much as I know. It's got something to do with a submarine launched missile with an X-ray laser warhead. The laser is pumped by a small nuclear-fission explosion and is multiply aimable to knock down missiles—presumably Soviet missiles—at a great range. Just thinking a missile like this up isn't illegal. If they really *built* one, maybe. Then again, with all the improvement in relations, any suggestion of one would be embarrassing."

Ned wrote notes in a reporter's notebook. "Mmm. That's it?"

"Except for details of size, throw weight, orbit, general location of the boomer—the picket submarine—detection by infrared satellite and communication to base by various satellite nets, all of which I have and most of which is at least alluded to in the layout, that's it."

"Does this information address the subject of your story?"

"Intimately."

"Does it bring a special light of understanding to bear?"

"Yes."

"You must remember this my boy: Even in a time of opening harmony there are men who feel their patriotism demands increased vigilance, an aggressive stance. Is it sidelight ideas that could detract from the narrative of the story as written?"

"I don't think so."

"Is it an exclusive with us? Is no one else covering this subject?"

"No other magazine is covering it. I don't know about these damn spooks. Anyone could have put the pieces together . . ."

"No. You did. You put the pieces together from where?"

"From other stories, from unclassified sources, from *Aviation Weekly*, for Christ's sakes, from our consultants on other stories about satellites and submarines and such. Anyone could . . ."

"No. This is yours, and now it's our scoop. You know how Stone loves to scoop the others."

"What should I do, Ned?"

"If you were a decorator, your job would be simple: Keep out of it. Especially since you don't know what you're onto. But you aren't. You're a journalist, a talented giver of facts. You have no choice, Charlie. Run with it, make it the best story you can."

"I'm worried."

"Why?"

"They could get rough."

"How rough?"

"My researcher, Murray, went to check some of the facts at Naval Ops, and I haven't heard from him since. How would I know? Am I a spook? Are you?"

"Yes, I see your problem. It's possible your researcher is being detained. It's possible he's been hit by a crosstown bus. You know how they are in this benighted town. I am not a father, at least not to my knowledge, and so I don't know what to tell you."

"You already told me. This is a story, Ned. I run with it, and that's that."

"Not all of it. The other part is knowing when to duck."

"You must have been good at that."

Edward Everett Crocker, seventy-two and survivor of many earthquakes, uprisings, and not a few coup attempts, rose grandly to fill his tweed suit. "Here I am," he said with irrefutable logic.

Chapter 8

Petrov Kruskin appeared at Charlie's house on time, three o'clock. He wore a jogging suit, gray, and new Nike air-support shoes. "Good evening, Charlie. I have been looking forward to our run, yes? Where do we go?"

"Have you been on the towpath?"

"I have only heard of it. I have not been on it. Sounds like a good plan for a place to run, so let's do it. But first, this is an interesting house with many treasures, all nautical. You are an expert sailor?"

"Just a sailor."

Petrov's eyes scanned the rooms, devouring them. He seemed to be surveying for a new building to fit within these walls. He looked at the locks on the back door and the catches on the window, "You think these locks give securing in such a society, Charlie?"

"Hell, Petrov. Nothing here to steal. Any good thief can see that."

"Paintings, artifacts, antiques of good quality. Plenty, Charlie."

"Christ, you'll get me scared. There are a few good paintings and prints, and maybe two good antiques out of the bunch, but it's difficult to separate the significant from the merely interesting."

"Even so. You need a dead-bolt lock back there. And simple lock on windows."

A Soviet expert on American security. Great. "Let's hit the bricks, Comrade Crimestopper."

Petrov shook his head at Charlie's inattention to good advice.

The towpath, a ten-minute drive toward the Potomac from Charlie's house, was almost deserted on this weekday afternoon. A few women walking dogs, an elderly couple with a pair of binoculars and a bird book. They left Charlie's car at Fisher's Boat-house and walked across the canal on the low wooden footbridge. Charlie used the end of the handrail to brace his stretches. Petrov was looking up and down the path.

"Few people at this time. Always this few?"

"I don't know." He lengthened his long back-leg muscles and tendons. "I guess so. Weekends, there are a lot of people walking and running and biking. Okay, you ready?"

"Of course."

Arrogant bastard. Charlie tied a rolled bandanna around his forehead.

"How many miles you want to do, Petrov?"

"However. What you want to do, I'll do."

"Mmm." Charlie switched the mode on his digital watch to "Starter" and hit the button. They started north. They would go for time, twenty out and twenty back. Petrov was stocky, but in running clothes Charlie could see that he was in good shape. His head and shoulders floated effortlessly above his springy stride; his eyes swept ahead of them. The day was overcast but mild. The leaves planed down around them, some of them touching the water's surface at the end of the last arabesque. Sweat began to prickle on Charlie's temples, and the rhythm set in. They had a long curve of the canal to themselves, and the fragrance of the leaves was the autumn's best scent.

"This was a great engineering accomplishment in its day, this canal," Charlie said, spacing his phrases with breathing. "To open the West beyond the Appalachian Mountains, beyond Cumberland."

Two young men swept past them, going south on bikes. In the acute sensitivity that sometimes comes with a runner's concentration on his effort, Charlie noticed that the Hispanic's rear brake touched the bowed rim of its tire and squeaked at every turn.

"There was a big lift-over at Cumberland ridge. Oxen and wagons and what-all. Freight got over the divide, got put on another canal that went down to the Ohio. Big medicine then."

"Obsolete before it was finished, yes?" Petrov knew about it, then. "Often happens. Great government project, subsidized by taxes, promoting trade with frontiers. Simpler technology arrives just as long project is finished. Railroads. Left with low-grade carrier of bulk goods, low priorities, commodities not needing fast delivery."

Okay, you Russian smartass, no more history for you. And he wasn't even breathing hard. They single-filed and moved right, hearing more bicycles coming up behind them.

One wheel squeaked.

Charlie turned and saw the knife a few feet away. "Petrov!" If he had been walking, he might have frozen and the blade would have caught him just under the rib cage. As it was, he kept moving, off course, looking back at the awful blade, and fell into the canal.

He pushed back into the water, which he did not feel as cold or hot or anything. He pushed away from the knives, since both men were off their bikes now, and holding double-edged knives low. They did not look like cooking knives, Charlie thought inanely.

Petrov had ducked and rolled once. He was up in a half-crouch, assessing the situation. *What the hell kind of engineering solution will he make of this? Oh, Jesus.*

There was only a moment of stasis, though it seemed like two or three minutes of silent negotiation. The Hispanic turned away from Petrov and started toward Charlie, while the black began to sway and look for the simplest opening to Petrov's liver. Charlie backpaddled out into the middle of the canal, hoping for some salvation that was better than swimming for Georgetown. He was six yards away from the knot of three people and saw it all clearly.

The Hispanic began to clamber down the slippery bank, carefully, to join Charlie in the water. Petrov watched him and watched the black. Petrov rose out of his crouch and walked toward the black as if he were walking across Sixteenth Street, purposefully, balanced, wary of traffic. The black lunged. Petrov pivoted like a man throwing a Frisbee, and the black tripped, cried out, and rolled into the brush at the far side of the towpath. Another inappropriate thought came to Charlie: *That's poison ivy.*

The Hispanic had reached the water's edge. Petrov turned to him and brought his hand up, holding, from somewhere— where did he hide that thing?—a small, flat automatic about the size of a tape cassette. Immediately, there was a sharp snap. The Hispanic flinched, hesitated with confused eyes fixed on Charlie, and fell face forward into the water.

Petrov looked back at the black getting up out of the poison ivy, considered an instant, and turned back to the Hispanic beginning to jerk facedown in the water. He brought his hand up again, and there was the snap. Charlie could see where the slug caught the back of the floating man's neck just under the skull. He could even see the ejected cartridge spin through the air and hear it ping on the stones of the towpath. *My God, Jesus, oh shit, Charlie.* The blood in the brown-green water was dark.

The black was halfway to Petrov now, holding his knife back for a thrust. Petrov turned and waited in the same pedestrian way, then did a nimble little skip at the moment before Charlie or the black expected it. He had the knife hand up and the little automatic under an ear, and there was hardly a snap this time, more a slap, and Petrov let the body fold stiffly to the gravel path, taking the knife carefully before it touched the ground. He walked to the edge of the canal above the Hispanic's body, shaking his head, frowning.

"Charlie," he called.

"Yes?"

"You swim?"

"Yeah. I swim."

"You're fine, then?"

"Yeah."

"Good. That's important. Look, Charlie, we've got to get out of here, you know? Come over here and do me a dumb favor. It's a little difficult. I'd do it, but it's cold, okay? Just under this hoodlum, here, is his knife. I think I see it. Get that, will you? And right back here," he patted the small of his back, "his knife sheath and a little pistol like so. That too, okay? Then we get you back and warm. Get you a drink of vodka."

Charlie nodded. He would do it, but he didn't know why. He swam to the body and ducked down, finding the nasty thing, with its wicked symmetry and sawteeth at the hilt. He got the things Petrov asked for and climbed up.

Petrov was crouched down, looking for something. "Sure, here we go. Found it. Got all three now." He held up three spent cartridges. "We can go. Same way we came, jog nice and easy. You're cold, you're going to . . . what is the idiom here? You're into shock soon. Not to worry. I'm right here, you know?"

Charlie didn't know. He didn't know why or what or when. They started back toward the boathouse, and he tried to look back once at the bodies, but Petrov said, "No, Charlie. That's all done. All done, Charlie. Run now, hot shower and a drink up there ahead. You got to make dinner for your kids and me, yes?"

At the car, Charlie took his key from the little pocket of his running shorts but stood dumbly in front of the door. Petrov took the key from his hand and led him around to the passenger side, unlocked the door, and guided Charlie's head safely under the brow of the roof.

Sitting in the driver's seat of Charlie's old Volvo station wagon, Petrov looked over the controls and fiddled with the steering-wheel lock before starting the engine. Charlie opened the door again, leaned out against his seat belt, and threw up, spitting and clearing his throat and coughing. He closed the door again and looked straight ahead.

"Charlie?"

Charlie nodded: "Okay, go, I'm all right."

Petrov pulled out of their parking space and drove up the ramp to Canal Road. "Charlie, what is rule on Canal Road at six-thirty? We got a one-way at this time?"

"Left," he replied, looking straight ahead.

Petrov turned left and drove along the canal to the foot of Arizona. He turned up the grade and chatted to Charlie in a tone that was meant to be reassuring. "Look, Charlie, those were bad fellows. Meant to kill you, you know. You got to be careful now. We got to keep you safe. And your children, too."

Charlie looked at Petrov sharply. "No one's going to hurt my children."

"No, Charlie. No one."

"Come on, Kruskin. Step on the gas and get me home."

"It's okay, Charlie. Someone's with your children right now."

Another sharp look.

"You got a good friend, Charlie. I'm going to stop at this phone there for just a minute, yes? Not worrying. Sit and relax, try to be warm, and we'll go home right away.' Petrov pulled over and reached into a bag on the back seat for his change. He got out and took the key with him.

Charlie watched him dial a pay phone, talk for thirty seconds, and walk back to the car. *Who is he? What is he in all this? He is not an engineer on a junket. How does Nikolai know him? How much does everyone know about me?* Charlie felt exposed, the dream of wandering onstage without clothes while the violinist is playing "Ave Maria." Charlie felt childish, helpless, hopeless against people who wore nasty automatics under their running shorts. But he was beginning to feel angry.

"This is the alley," Charlie said.

"Charlie, I got alleys even in Moscva. Alleys this Kruskin knows, raised in alleys. Almost home now, right? Okay, we'll leave your car here. Needs a job on the valves, I think. You hear those tappings? We're going to walk up the alley without talking and walk in the back door."

"Why?"

"Little complication. Nothing. Taken care of."

Charlie did not like the sound of "complication," and he

liked "taken care of" even less. But they walked up the alley that had once seemed so benign, Kruskin with a gym bag full of God knows what—bombs, tanks, poison-tipped arrows. The back door was open, but as soon as they came in, Nikolai stepped from the back room. He had watched them come into the yard.

"Little brother! What hardships you are having! My dear friend." Nikolai's arms in his expensive suit went around Charlie's sodden sweatshirt and stayed there, as warming and as solid as before, but stranger, with Kruskin and his bag standing by. "First things in the first place, however. You will catch a death if we do not treat you well."

"Where are my children?"

"Doing homework. Although I think Mike is listening to too much rock-and-roll music to get much done, but this may be how he does work. He is in his room."

"Sarah?"

"Was at . . . He took a scrap of paper from his vest pocket. "At Elana's. Not to worry. Someone picked her up. She is upstairs."

"Who?"

"A friend of mine. And of Kruskin's."

Nikolai was pouring a glass half full of Moscovskaya vodka. It had been in the freezer, and it had a syrupy sheen swirling into the bottom of the tumbler. "Two things. Your responsibilities now are simple. Later not simple. Now, two: drink this, one. Other is, get into hot shower and dry things. Then we talk. One little matter first." He put his arm around Charlie and walked him, choking on a deep draft of cold vodka, to the front hall, stopping him as they reached the entrance to the living room. Nikolai held out his hand without looking and Petrov placed a pair of small binoculars into it. "Look through that window, Charlie, at a blue car on the opposite side of street, yes? Sure. You look here and tell me about recognizing man at steering wheel. Turn little knob for really clear picture. Take plenty of time, because he won't see us at this angle."

Nikolai turned to Kruskin and spoke to him in Russian. Charlie could not understand the words, but the tone translated well. He had never heard Nikolai use such a tone before; it was not at all unkind, not rude, but it was commanding. There was no question of persuasion in it, only a full expectation of complete compliance. When Charlie raised his head from the binoculars, he saw Kruskin, who had just killed two men—assassins, thugs, whatever—with skillful, frightening lack of difficulty nodding his head in a small bow to each of Nikolai's comments and orders. Charlie knew something about men and authority; it was not bureaucratic agreement Kruskin was showing, it was respect. Where was the real world? *What happened?*, he asked himself. *I have fallen through the looking glass.* He handed the binoculars back to Nikolai and started up the stairs.

"You know him, Charlie?"

"No."

"Good. Better. That would be really too complicated." Nikolai laughed, and the two Soviets shared niceties in Russian, laughing harder. *Oh, boy,* Charlie thought, *Charlie Salt's Soviet Bloc Spy Parlor.*

"Schottsie." He stuck his head inside Mike's door.

"Alphonse. Doing my homework, Dad."

"Turn the music down, will you, sport? Everything okay?"

"Great. Nikolai helped me with my history. He said the book's all wrong."

"What period are you working on?"

"First World War."

"Trust the book. Nikolai's got an ax to grind."

"Ax?"

"Finish your homework. Get your hugger ready. I'm going to need one or two."

"How'd you get wet?" Mike was just noticing his damp condition.

"Fell into the canal."

"Oh, good go, Grace. Fred Astaire, Dad. You fell in the canal?" Giggles, with pointing finger. "Too much, dude. Sarah's got to hear this."

"You little sadist." No one was going to hurt Mike. No one was going to hurt Sarah. Now he was angry.

"Look at this, Sarah." Mike had run up the stairs ahead of him. Charlie entered her attic room looking like a muskrat. "Look, twinkletoes is bouncing along on the towpath, trips on a cockroach, and falls in the canal. How may runners do you think fall in the canal?" He turned to Charlie. "We're doing statistics at school, Dad. What do you think? Less than one percent?"

"How may smartassed twelve-year-olds are thrown down the stairs before they're sent off to military school?" Charlie gave him a fake grimace that nevertheless meant, Get back to work. Mike kissed him, avoiding the cold sweatshirt, "Ooh, you throw up, Dad? You've got to brush teeth. Sorry."

"It's okay, sport. See you later."

Mike rumbled down the stairs.

"Dad, you've got to get into the shower." Sarah shook her head. "You all right?"

"Just wet."

"I mean, are you all right? What's the trouble?"

"Any trouble here? Did anything happen here?' He felt anxiety come up in his throat and tried to control it, but she knew him too well.

"No, that's not what I meant. Are you getting hypo . . . hypo . . .

"Hypothermic."

"Yeah. Are you?"

"Probably a little. I'm a little edgy because of it. Things okay with Nikolai?"

"He's nice. He came to Elena's with two friends, and they left when we got here. Is he an important man at the embassy?"

"Yes."

"I thought so, the way they talk to him. He really likes you, Dad."

Charlie nodded. "Get your homework done. I'll start dinner."

"What's for dinner?"

He didn't answer.

The shower was, as always, his refuge, though he sometimes heard small cries and strange music in its steamy roar.

Kruskin was opening cans of soup, sniffing at them in approval. He was apparently fond of opening cans because he had opened garbanzo beans and peas and hominy, as well. Charlie was moving slowly; he felt stiff without the pain of stiffness. *Nerves, fright, confusion. It's a wonder I don't get it over with and pee my pants.* Kruskin was about to open a can of peaches. "Petrov, we won't need those for soup."

"Oh. Sure. Good can opener, Charlie."

Nikolai began to speak in Russian, in a low and friendly voice a superior might use with a young favorite. He caught himself in midsentence and began again in English. "Put on the water, Kruskin. Tea for warming inside of Charlie. Outside now looking better, but inside always comes along behind." He sat at the big butcher-block surface with a small glass of vodka before him looking like an uncle who has seen too much of the world, waiting and regretting the necessity of telling it to a child.

Charlie took down a Calfalon three-quart saucepan and emptied a can of pepper pot soup into it, then a can of consumme. He drained and added the peas and garbanzos and a small bowl of leftover rotini in the refrigerator. He followed them with two healthy glugs of medium-dry sherry. Kruskin had the can opener and was looking through the pantry. What would he open next?

Charlie added water to the soup, stirred it, and sat down across from Nikolai. They looked at each other. Nikolai smiled; Charlie did not.

"How's your credit card, Charlie?"

Charlie shook his head as if he'd been dealt a glancing blow from a passing boomerang. "Comrade Tsiokolvsky. What the billy-fuck is a Soviet Socialist doing asking me about credit cards, which are certainly a western banking plot to snare the people?"

"But very convenient, yes? Not to worry, I'm sure, but being on the safe side, we should get Mike and Sarah out of town for some small time. I know you will miss them and they need their father, most especially Mike needs his father, but . . ."

"Stop. Back up. Look at me, Nick."

Nikolai's head tilted to the side as he looked, still smiling.

"Nick, I'm an art director, an explainer. I live in a world of ideas. I'm pretty far away from hands-on life. My wife is dead. I live in my work and those kids up there. I don't touch the real stuff anymore. Now. Now I almost get disembow- eled, I fall in the canal, and I watch your engineer friend ice the two movie stars that tried to kill me. This is too much for an abstract guy, Nick. I'm about to drop the ball. What the fuck is going on? There's a guy watching my house, just like I suspected in what I hoped was a paranoid delusion, and Murray Hofnung is missing . . ."

Something tart and bitter had changed in Nikolai's face. "What? What do you know about Murray?"

"You won't like it, Charlie. We talk about Murray, and we don't think he comes back to you. You think a lot of him, right?"

"Right. Like . . . like a younger brother. Right."

"Okay, little brother of mine. Nick tells you everything he knows . . ."

"Wait. You're not really the cultural secretary of the embassy, are you?"

"Sure I am, good one."

"But you're something more."

"So? I'm ambitious. We talk about this culture I live in, Charlie, many nights. Building up base of support and building up favors, being part of right organizations. Same as corporate power basing . . . Right term?"

"You're KGB. You're a spy."

"You're crazy man. You look at me, now. Is Nick a spy? You know what that 'spy' word means? Nothing. Your journalists, Jack Anderson and Woodstein, better spies than whole damn network of Soviet spies. Open up more secret drawers, Charlie."

"You're KGB."

"Yes," Nick said, finally exasperated with Charlie's refusal to listen. "Yes, and very good at this, too, as well as good cultural secretary. I am good intelligence man, Charlie. Analyst, gatherer of information, listener. What I tell you? Better both sides look more, worry less. Open up, talk, look, spy down with satellites, listen to rumblings under test sites together. Release tensions. Listen, crazy Charlie, you better damn be glad Nick is a good intelligence man, because you got a problem. You better damn be glad Petrov is one fine damn field man, or kids are orphans this bad night. You think I'm getting secret of White House toilet from you, put in fake peanut butter jar, smuggle to Finland, across border by cross-country ski to Mother Russia? Huh? You got Nick in prison, now, shot in morning, one last cigarette, don't even smoke? Someday I go back to Moscva and they will say, 'Nick did good job of listening, of giving us true picture of country we compete with but need. Nick did his good work. Never got secret of White House toilet but, you know, bigger broader secrets of what society is up to, what technology is up to, these are less spectacular and more important. So we'll give him a small medal, this big, and maybe a small dacha. Hard worker.' Nothing huge, Charlie. Nothing as good as what you will have, which is millions of people knowing how things work because you explain."

"Listen to us, Petrov." He turned to the younger man fixing tea in a pot. "We go on like this evening and evening. Philosophical dispute. I love this man, Petrov,"Nikolai looked back at Charlie with concern, "but he is crazy and needs hard help now, and he is not opening his ears."

"My ears are open far enough. Tell me, Nick, and simply please, what beehive have I stuck my hand into, and what got you involved, and how can I get out of it and get back to my old life."

"Philosophy again, little brother. If your ears are open, listen to Uncle Vanya talk to you completely aside from this crisis. Don't go back to old life. Go back to real life. Start your life again. Get laid. Care."

"Cut the Plato, Nick. Give me the poop."

"Sure." Nikolai drank a sip of the vodka. "Probably when your good researcher Murray goes to Pentagon to verify research and they are hearing about your story, they want to find out how much you know, why? Maybe some small intelligence group, outlaw group hiding inside the normal intelligence structure, develops this thing further than anyone knows, maybe they make X-ray laser missile already. Not good to be known when treaty is being renegotiated. Anyway, they try to break into your office to see how much you got but run into guard and stupidly kill him. This is stupid business."

"Then why did Petrov kill those two guys?"

"Charlie, you are good liberal soul, but those two guys were trying real hard to kill you. Would try again. We slow their controllers down and back them off just a little. Guard at *Geographic* was not trying to kill the hoodlums that came for your stuff. Maybe they were practicing for you. I don't know, but these are bad men. Not even desperate, you know? Phrase comes up at the White House all the time: 'Playing hardball.' Means not to pay attention to rules of decency. That's what we got. Not an easy game. You're lucky you got friends."

"You're my friend, Nick. Sure enough. But I have to ask you what your controllers have invested in this. Petrov came in from out of town, and at least two others are involved."

"Oh, more than two, Charlie. Okay. Here's trouble for me and for you. Where my uncles are involved is in the same layout. I told them about it. I went on your limb with you because you need help. I said, 'There is something here that worries Pentagon. Something they want to keep secret. Maybe they don't play fair at Geneva.' They said, 'Can you get it published?' This would be a great embarrassment to your administration, in their eyes. Some kind of treaty bargaining leverage . . . not all of us are Gorbachev. I said, 'I can't, but Charlie sure is trying, and they will stop him.' They said, "Protect Charlie and get it published.' So, we protect you, and you get it published."

"Just a goddamned minute. I'm not publishing anything on Moscow's orders."

"No. You wouldn't. But you had a reason to publish this in the first place, didn't you?"

"Absolutely."

"Still?"

"Yes, but presented the way we want to present it."

"Not my concern. Not Moscva's. After publication, if we find something wrong, Moscva will say what it can. We open it up to whole world and let air in. Worst thing would be hoodlum groups making these things themselves in secret."

"I've got no obligation to Moscow."

"Or to me, Charlie. Only obligation you got is to come and visit me in my dacha, if day comes. You get free of these guys and I'm happy. Your life is good Soviet investment."

"How do I get free of these guys? We can't kill all of them."

"Only way I could think of is obvious. Publish. After that, whatever it is, they don't care about you but only about protecting themselves, getting away."

"So I just get it published?"

"Difficult?"

"I'm not the publisher. But what about the guy in the blue car outside? What about the kids?"

"Blue car is gone now. Somebody is watching from somewhere else. Maybe two guys. For a while, you will live with this business. Now we get Mike and Sarah to safety. These guys would try to take them, and maybe, to make you do what they want. Tell me, you know anyone who would take them . . . someone not expected, like they would expect your sister or something? Got to be someone who takes them without questions, far away."

"Yes."

"Who? Where?"

Charlie hesitated.

"You got to trust me, Charlie. Trust Nick."

"How about . . .," Charlie began, but Nikolai held up his hand and swept an enigmatic finger around the possibly bugged walls, smiling as if it were an elaborated arranged game. He drew a small notebook from his jacket pocket and gave Charlie a ballpoint pen. Charlie wrote "John Carter-Bath, Maine? Could pick up at Portland airport." Nikolai nodded.

"I'll get their work from their school—"

"Forget social improvements until this is over. Give them a break."

"What do I tell them?"

"I don't know. Tell them what a good father would tell them. I am good cultural secretary, good intelligence chief, not good father."

"Good uncle, though."

"Yes, and good big brother. don't you forget."

Petrov put the teapot down in front of them with bowls of soup and spoons. Nikolai spoke to him in Russian, and he took bowls up the stairs to Sarah and Mike. Nikolai punched a seven-digit number into the phone and spoke in Russian, then in a language Charlie had never heard, a slurred, dense tongue. He hung up.

"They will call me back with the numbers of possible flights." He saw the quizzical look on Charlie's face. "Yes, that was not Russian at all, you know. That was a dialect they will find difficult to follow. Just slows them down."

Charlie shook his head. "Sit down and have some soup, Nick."

Charlie, Charlie. he said to himself. *Who do I have to fuck to get out of this mess!*

$\triangledown$

Chapter 9

CARLTON DEAUVILLE WAS ONE tough son of a bitch. Had to be. Inspector in the Homicide Division, the elite of the beat, the force force. Other divisions dealt with traffic offenders and second-story men; homicide dealt with killers.

Deauville knew that the truth was not as colorful as the image. Homicide required a thoughtful mind, an ability to sort facts, and a way of distancing yourself from death in many forms. Wife stabbing, child abuse, drug OD's, bar fights, suicides, old people dying alone in their sleep, every "suspicious" death in the city came to homicide. The toughest part of a homicide cop was his stomach.

One of those nights, Deauville said to himself. It was still early, but he could see it coming. He could see it coming as he pulled up in front of the apartment house. Scout car pulled up, lights flashing, coroner's wagon, neighbors and gawkers keeping back, away from the tide of people going in and out of the building, evidence units, supervisor, medical examiner. The faces of the people were enough to tell him, but the medical examiner gave it to him officially.

"Carlton." He was hanging his badge on his jacket pocket, arranging it just so.

"Dr. Finn, how's it going tonight?"

"Up to this point, great. Downhill after this. You got a bad one here. A couple of Smelly Dave's. Looks like a couple of queers rode out on some bad coke. Dead maybe four days, five. Apartment building is fairly new: good venting, well-sealed. No one smelled it until last night, and by this morning it was really bad. Good luck. Take a quick look; I'd like to get the meat in the cooler so we can run some tests, at least. How long you want?"

"About half a second."

"That's all you'll want, I promise."

"Give me ten minutes."

"I'll be here."

Carlton got his briefcase out of his car and walked into the lobby with it. "Officer?" he said to a patrolman.

"Apartment four-oh-six, sir. And sir? I'd—"

"I know, officer, I've done this before."

"Sorry, sir."

In the elevator, he opened the briefcase and took out his small jar of Vick's Vaporub. He took two dabs of the pungent gel and wiped it into his nostrils, then closed the jar and put it away in his briefcase quickly before the door opened again. It wouldn't cut it all, but it would help. He'd learned that from one of the old boys. The elevator door opened, and he knew it would help only a little.

"Carlton, good to see you," Bunkie Austin shook his hand. He was smiling but he looked pale and one cheek twitched. "Let's wrap this up and get the bodies out of here, okay?" The corridor was crowded with uniforms and suits.

"Quick as I can. Anything I ought to know?"

"All the barf in the kitchen sink is from our boys. Nothing else unusual."

"Prints?"

"What we could. His barf is in the sink too."

"I might as well see the elephant."

"Don't lose it, Carlton."

"Have I ever, Burkie?" He walked in like *one tough son of a bitch. Tough talker,* Carlton thought.

Small living room. Coffee table set with two glasses, almost empty bottle of scotch, six Newport Light butts in a saucer. No peanuts, no crackers. He looked at the sound system; no tape in the player, no disk on the turntable. Radio set to a classical station but turned off. One coat on a chair, leather with a cheap ruff. Nothing on the rug.

To the right, in the kitchen, the acid stench of vomit competed with decay. Carlton looked in the refrigerator. It was neat and only half used. Perrier, sparkling apple cider, machine-squeezed orange juice half empty. English muffins, butter, jam, organic peanut butter, cheese, oranges, apples, grapefruits, acidophilus milk, vitamins and supplements in the door. Health nut.

Except for the sink full of vomit, the kitchen was white and clean. Deauville leaned down and smelled the towel hung on the small oven's door handle. Clean. He began opening cupboards.

"Inspector, are you fooling around in here for some reason? We're waiting to cart these stiffs away to the cooler."

"Take your time, son. I'll be there in a shake." He could say "son" to this whitebread morgue tech and put him off for five minutes. He was fifteen years older. And there was something wrong here. He finished the cupboard and didn't find what he was looking not to find. He loosened his collar and noticed how hot it was.

The thermometer was in the living room, set to eighty-seven. No one had noticed because of the smell and the tension of having two rotting corpses ten feet away, but it was stifling.

Okay, let's view the deceased.

Deauville took out a notepad from his briefcase and a ballpoint from his jacket pocket. Two male corpses in advanced state of decay. *We all black brothers after four, five days dead,* Deauville thought. Mottled skin, dark purplish brown. Fluids of decomposition apparent on mattress and floor. And in a black streak across and down the abdomen of the corpse on its back, where the head of the other corpse lay weeping its fluids. It would be difficult to move these two and keep the skin intact.

Both mouths were drawn back in the last joke, the *risus sardonicus,* a sickly smile of mirthless jest; have you heard the one about death?

Deauville had dipped his head almost immediately. It was always like this, his gorge rising. The hat protected him, its brim coming down and shielding his eyes from the mutilated children, the piles of old flesh, the cut and violated bodies, and protecting him from his colleagues' eyes seeing his weakness. Deauville, the tough stud killer driller, Deauville be one mother fuck tough sonofabitch, Jack. It took only a moment, then he was ready to look up for a moment.

He began to look around the room. Neat, laid out sensibly. A tiny vial, and the paraphernalia of cocaine with it: mirror, razor blade, rolled bill. The proximal cause. Large bookcase with a large percentage of nonfiction: biographies and science commentary. Yellow pads beside the bed with notes on some research project. Polaroids: women, a brunette, a blonde, a dark-haired woman, and another blonde. Framed picture signed "Love and hugs, Bonnie."

"You have names on these birds?" he asked.

"One definite, one possible. This one, the one with dark

hair, lives here. Name of Murray Hofnung."

Deauville lowered his hat brim, and his eyes shifted rapidly between the foot of the bed and the feet of the patrolman.

"Here's his wallet. The other may be one . . ." the patrolman consulted his notes, "Judd Penn, an amateur hooker around P Street Beach. One of the guys thinks he recognizes him. Hard to tell. No ID on him. That's about it."

Deauville opened the wallet and turned past the license and bank cards to the pocket for business cards. He took one out carefully: "Murray J. Hofnung, Researcher, Magazine Art, *National Geographic Society.*"

He was standing in the bathroom when the morgue tech spoke to him again. "You all done with the stiffs?"

"They're all yours. Have a good time."

He heard them breathing hard and grunting in displeasure as they maneuvered one body, then another into bags. They would be wearing their brown rubber gloves and their red rubber aprons and their farm boots. Everyone else would be out of the room and down the hall.

Bathroom neat: one towel, one toothbrush. Toilet kit with razor, deodorant, comb, brush, fingernail clippers. Compartment under the kit with seven condoms. No condoms on the bodies.

Deauville knew that he could make no generalizations about homosexuals or bisexuals, especially not when it came to homicide. But the pattern wasn't adding up here. A health nut with no booze in the apartment except one bottle of cheap scotch. He hadn't found any other liquor in the cabinets. Unlikely; where there is one bottle of booze, there are other bottles with it, liqueurs or gin or club soda. Pictures of several women, of one special woman. Could be a closet queen, a weekend warrior. He buys acidophilus milk but also buys unreliable coke. Unlikely. Compulsively neat, but his clothes are piled in the corner with the hooker's, both together. Not laid on the chair but thrown in one spot not two. Keeps his vitamins and supplements in the refrigerator to maintain the potency, but doesn't use a condom fucking a street whore like Penn. Could be part of the excitement. The temperature; why was it set so high? So they could prance around in their Underalls? Could it be to promote a rapid decay and early discovery? Why?

But add to all that *National Geographic*. Deauville did not like coincidence, and he did not believe in psychics. How did Mr. Charles Salt know that Murray was in trouble? What are the odds against two men who work near each other, a guard and a researcher, dying within a week by suspicious causes?

Shit, this was going to be sticky and difficult, and probably someone would get his head caught in the shredder before it was done. He hated coincidence. There was no coincidence, really. Just a tangled mat of causes that were difficult to follow up.

He made some real notes on his pad and started out, taking one last look around and wondering who comes in to clean up after a mess like this. The curtains would have to be burned, probably the rugs, the bed, most of the clothes. The smell was still deep and disgusting.

$\triangledown$

Chapter 10

NIKOLAI NODDED TO THE messenger from the embassy, smiling. He closed the back door and took out his notebook. He wrote it down and showed it to Charlie: "Delta 1146, 9:45—change Boston Logan same terminal—Downeast 668, 10:55, arr 11:35.

"Sorry not much time for good sleep for children;"

"They'll survive. They're more resilient than we are."

"Most true. Can you arrange this with your friend?"

Charlie started for the phone.

"No, Charlie, not for anything like this. Once again, those guys got too much opportunity to plant devices, yes? We got to call somewhere else."

"Pay phone on the corner."

Nikolai turned his head sideways and squinched his eyes. "Not to alarm, little brother, but pay phone on corner is very exposed. Old training from clock-with-dagger spy like me." He smiled broadly. *Nick, you are one of the world-class con men.*

"How about my phone at work? I could drive down, drive directly into the underground lot, and take the elevator up. Security's been beefed up since the killing. Besides that, I'd better get the damned layout—"

"It's at office." Nikolai was concerned.

"Yes, along with what I'll need to work on it tonight if I'm going to sell it to the Stone. He Who Must Be Obeyed is not convinced we truly need this layout. Cartography is trying to replace it with a world map of missile tracks, and the shooter—"

"Shooter?"

"The photographer, Jillian Ansara, wants to scrap it for a dusk shot of a laser test."

"This is too much. You must be assertive."

"I must be political. I must be persuasive. This is where you and Petrov and the whole Politburo can't help me, Nick, not with John Wheeler Stone. The Cherubim and the arch-angels in their degree do not sway the Stone. He moves at his whim only. Ned Crocker said that in Seventy-eight, Stone was out at his place tending his figs and vines when the sky opened up and the voice of God boomed out: "John, you should change the lead on the St. Sophia story.'"

"So? What did the Stone editor do?"

"He said, "Okay, I'll think about it.' He did. Then he killed the story. Said he didn't like the shoot and didn't like PR pressure either."

"You got trouble here, Charlie?"

"Not if I get to work and stop playing everyone else's game. I'll drive down and get the stuff, my friend, and arrange for the kids. Be back in forty minutes.

"Petrov will walk you to the car."

Petrov appeared with one of Charlie's dishtowels, ruined with graphite and oil as he finished the stripping of a small automatic. "Here, Charlie, you ever use one of these things?"

"Ak. Not one of those. Just a target pistol, a Ruger .22, a long time ago."

"Good, good. All same. Real simple, this one, little Walther. Makes a big boom, that's what you want. Here is safety, yes? Off, on. Here is hammer, which you will not need; just pull trigger first time and hammer works. When you shoot this thing, ever, put hammer back like this, so not to blow your foot off. Tucks back here real nice." He put it in Charlie's belt at the small of his back. "Feel like Clint Eastwood, Charlie?"

"No. More like Charlie Chaplin."

He normally took Massachusetts down to Seventeenth, past the embassies and through Sheridan Circle with Phil Sheridan flamboyantly waving to him. Tonight, though, he took Rock Creek Park and drove to the river and past the Kennedy Center and the Lincoln and the Jefferson monuments. The lights of the monuments comforted him.. If he was going to live in a city, he might as well get the benefit of the show. He had to think, too.

He drove up Independence, annoyed at his Volvo for driving rough, but still thinking. *So I'm back in fifty minutes.* He turned north on Fourteenth to head for *Geographic*, but went east at Constitution Avenue to visit his favorite monument, lonely and neglected General Grant at the head of the Mall. Just past the Museum of American History, he began to swear at the Volvo. It stopped with a gasp, and he clutched, put it in neutral, and coasted to the curb in front of the Natural History Museum.

It was supposed to stop three miles earlier. The crimped fuel line was poorly done, but a certain amount of hurry had been involved.

As the car stopped, Charlie noticed that the car behind his pulled over with him. He sat, waiting. Nothing. Charlie got out, and the car door opened too. Trying to feel the automatic in his belt, Charlie walked quickly around the front of his car and joined a stream of people moving into the Museum for a lecture. A man got out of the Chevrolet behind Charlie's car, readjusted his belt and jacket, and followed him in.

The guards were busy with the crowd. Charlie slipped away from them and up the stairs. He knew immediately it was a mistake. The light was dim, only bright enough to let the maintenance people move along with their sighing machines. *Get out of here, Charlie. Up the stairs and out the other door.*

No. He thought of the other side, the Mall, dark and windy, lined with trees; no, the wrong environment for a terrified art director. He thought he heard something on the stairs below, and he kept climbing up to the Mall entrance level under the rotunda. At the far side of the big elephant, two men were cleaning benches and laughing with deep chocolate voices. Keep moving. He found the next stairs and started up them to find Roger Johnson's office. It was the only office he knew here; Roger was an old friend and had been a consultant for one of his dinosaur stories. He would get in the office somehow and call Petrov and . . . There were definitely footsteps coming up the stairs now. A man with a tweed jacket and gray hair came into the rotunda. He scanned the space, and his eyes fixed on Charlie for a moment longer than necessary. Charlie turned and continued to walk up the stairs as coolly as he could make himself.

I'm walking like I've got a stick in my ass, take it easy. Sure, Charlie, take it the fuck easy. You're really at home with people trying to kill you. This thought scared him properly, and when he turned the corner of the stairs he ran up the next flights as fast as he could without sounding like the elephant was with him.

My God, a dim corridor. This is how they get it in a spy

movie, dim corridor, no way out. Does begging count? What if I promise to be good forever? God damn. Roger's door was locked; so was every other door he could try. *Quiet, quiet! Footsteps. Time to run like hell, Charlie.*

Where am I? He tried to remember how the architecture went. He had done a cross section of the building for a story on the Mall. *I'm two floors down from the mansard level and almost over the blue whale, and I'm petrified.* He noticed, though, that he was also excited. He bolted up another set of granite stairs and stopped at the landing. *Shit.*An old exhibit relegated to staff-only space: Eskimo skulls in the tertiary stages of syphilis. *Get out of here, Charlie.*

He was up on the curved galleries just under the rotunda. These were the best places to browse with a curator on a rainy morning. The white boxes. Twenty thousand of them stacked everywhere on this floor and others. Four by four by four, tight, filled with drawers or racks and containing treasures: collections of Eskimo cribbage boards, a hundred macaw pelts, wolfskins, the skulls of foxes. *Love to look another time,* Charlie noted to himself, *but right now I need an empty to hide in.*No such luck. Down one corridor, up another. *You're just about over the whale now. That wall ahead will be the enclosure of the skylight over it. The classic movie mistake, Salt. You went up, and you can't walk out of the building onto thin air. You're screwed.*

He kept moving, and there was another staircase. He took it, groped for a light at the top, and found the kind of surreal setting that refreshed his special mind.

Charlie, you've been playing everybody's game but yours.

Steve Burns was doing the dance. He was playing with Salt, cat and mouse. He moved along behind him, glimpsing him briefly, fairly certain that Salt had seen him only once, on the main floor. Every few minutes he would make a noise, perversely warning him, making him nervous. Not cruelly, but playing out his own skill, enjoying the field again. He was done playing; time to get this done and get home to his wife. This was the top floor; he was here. Good choice; the cleaning people had been here already, and the body wouldn't be found until early morning, the next shift of guards. Time, containment.

But he wasn't on this corridor. Where was he? A staircase. He moved toward it slowly. Burns smiled sweetly as he heard something being knocked over on the floor above. *Mr. Salt, good-bye.*

He used the staircase cautiously. No sense in rushing this to carelessness. His wife always told him when he left the house, "Be careful." She had told him that when he was a field man in the sixties and when he was a desk man in the early eighties, and she still cautioned him. *Maybe that's what's kept me safe all these years,* Burns mused as he worked the corners and angles of the stairs up into the dark, holding the revolver and silencer muzzle-up in both hands. Maybe.

It was dark, black. Some dim emanation came from a pool beyond the blackness. He crouched and moved forward, feeling with his left hand for a pillar or wall with a switch. Here. The banks of lights threw the place into stark brightness.

It was a scene from Hieronymos Bosch, a small static hell, an evil parody of Noah. The catwalk that ringed the milk-glass skylight above the great blue whale held a population of ruined taxidermy. Birds, beasts, fish, and early men stood, reclined, leaned, hung. Half a dozen tatterdemalion flamingos lay together like faded pink cordwood. A dusty American bison lifted its head from the pine prairie floor, realizing that its hump had been eaten away in the thirties. A poorly prepared chimp hung dejectedly from the sprinkler pipes, bemoaning its patch-eaten fur sagging in strips and its sawdust spilling out. Naked Cro-Magnons with bad fright wigs gazed together for game that would never come from the far side of the skylight. Wolves stood vigilantly, looking more like road kills raised from the dead. But the eyes! Hundreds of bright, inquisitive, keen glass eyes reflected the gleam of naked light bulbs, a hard and trying gaze of the dead, the neglected. Hello, Steve Burns, they said. He shuddered. He didn't like this place.

Then get it over with. He moved toward the far turn of the catwalk on the balls of his feet, turning unexpectedly at intervals. *Come on, Salt, make your mistake. I want to get out of here. Come on, you chickenshit son of a bitch. Come on.*

He would make a deal with him. He would be reasonable, give him safe conduct, then he would drop him at the stairs. At the corner of the catwalk, he rose to a reasonable posture. He let his revolver hang blandly at his side. He turned and faced the population of lepers.

"Mr. Salt," he began. "I don't want . . . "

One of the Cro-Magnon men thrust forward, plunging his flint-tipped spear into the small of Steve Burns's back. The flint edges cut through tweed jacket, cotton shirt, skin and muscle easily because the flint-knapping technology of the Cro-Magnon was highly developed. The gun dropped. Burns found he could not speak. He stepped forward. He groped behind him for the awful pain and tried to escape it, his legs still working, but he met the railing of the catwalk. All the eyes gleamed at him. He sagged down into a crouch, slowly, losing sight and balance in a great rushing in his ears, and then he went through the railing of the catwalk. Two panes of the milk glass, under the clear glass skylight above, shattered and fell to the hall below. Burns almost hung up on the glass supports but rotated free, falling twenty feet to the curving back of the great blue whale and sliding six feet toward the tail, with a splash and a smear of blood to mark his path.

Charlie looked over the railing to the gray-haired man lying on the whale. Milk glass littered the floor below it, but there was no commotion from below. Maybe one maintenance man thought it was another's accident. *And I thought the gun would make a fuss. In any case, Charlie, it's time to get your clothes on. It could be embarrassing to be caught naked, especially in this damn wig.*

He moved down the stairs as casually as he could, retracing his steps to the lower level and walking out with the same confusion of lecture students. It was not hard to get a cab on Independence, and there was one place he wanted to go. Safety, home: the Geographic.

$\triangledown$

Chapter 11

T HE GUARD GREETED HIM, looking up from a small TV. "Mr. Salt."

"Night shift, Elvin?"

"Everybody's doing every shift, Captain says. After Wheeler. And he says we got too damn lax, and he says we not just a bunch of kid-herders for Explorer's Hall, we are security men."

"What do you think about that?"

"Mr. Salt, if you was to, excuse me, break wind on the eighth floor up there this evening, there'd be one of us crinkling up his nose nearby. Yeah, we got too easy. Lot of important goods in this place, but the most important thing is you, and Mr. Crocker on seven, and Miss Ansara . . . you know? That's what we are, we're family. You have a good evening, now. Call me if you see anything, hear?"

"I rest easy, Elvin."

Elvin winked. "Not too damned easy, Mr. Salt."

He signed the night register by the elevators and noticed his hand was shaking. He tried to control it and make a presentable signature, but he couldn't.

The eighth floor. He was shaking harder now. He could feel muscles in his face tugging like insects. He wanted to

110

sit in his own chair, alone. He wanted Kim to hold him. He wanted to be working on a very hard story, calling home and telling Mike and Sarah to order a pizza and get their homework done because he was totally tied up. He wanted to work all night on something he knew well. He didn't want the gray-haired man to be sprawled on the blue whale or the guys on the towpath to be floating toward Georgetown. They weren't dead. They would get up and do something else, go home and watch TV, have dinner. They would play another game. But they were dead, and Charlie rubbed his hands for warmth as if winter had come to the eighth floor.

He passed his office and walked to the layout rooms. He wanted to see a story laid out on the wall. Chills passed over him.

He turned the corner and walked into the layout room and yelped, loudly, sadly, like a dog that has been locked in the barn. Jillian Ansara lay dead on the floor, her strong arms fallen outward, her dark face closed.

Charlie's bark scared the hell out of Jillian. She jackknifed up to her feet, shouting herself. "What the hell! What? What happened?" She looked around, pushed past Salt, and looked down the hall. Nothing but a guard dogtrotting toward them.

"Miss Ansara, everything all right?"

"Christ. How's your CPR, Davis? My heart stopped cold. I was resting on the floor, and I scared Charlie Salt, apparently. Then he scared the shit out of me."

"Oh, you be fine now." At their best, the guards had a paternal interest in the strange writers and artists that made up the Society. "You had a little fright, is all. Mr. Salt, there, he look like he got the worst of it. That so, Mr. Salt?"

Charlie did not look at either of them, but walked unsteadily toward his room.

"He'll be fine, Davis."

"You look in on him, make sure?" Davis asked.

"I'll take care of him."

She walked after Charlie. He sat down heavily in his dark room. She turned on a desk lamp, always aware of lighting. The lamp made the tears that were beading on his cheeks and soaking into his beard glisten. She found a tissue and gently blotted the tears. He looked up at her; his mouth was making words without sounds.

"Tell me," she said. *Tell me, Charlie. I'll catch you.* The desire to comfort Charlie surprised her.

"I killed a man."

She was already frowning in concern at Charlie's anxiety. She wheeled the nearest chair to face him close and took his hands in hers. "Charlie," she said, but nothing more. She looked at him steadily and nodded; "I'm here, go on."

"He was trying to kill me with a gun. Today. On the towpath today, two other men tried to kill me. Knives. They're dead. I didn't kill them. A Russian killed them, one, two, just like that." He looked up to her and stated the obvious. "I'm just not used to all this."

She floundered for a moment. Charlie Salt, the eccentric art director. He was a little crazy, they said. Sure, but was he making all this up? Killing?

Charlie cleared his throat. "I've run foul of some damned intelligence group at the Pentagon, some maverick bunch of crazies. I guessed too close to a secret, some forbidden project they're implementing. If I open up the project, it'll be very messy for them. I think Murray may be dead too. I'm not making this up. My kids are in danger. I've got to get them out of town. Can you help me?"

She looked at him a moment longer. "How?" she asked, the frown still on her face.

"Jesus. Give me another . . . I'll get it." He rose and blew his large nose. "Hark, the horn of Roland sounds to summon Charlemagne," he said to no one in particular. Maybe he was a little crazy. But in Jillian's family, emotion was measured out in hard pills to be taken silently. If there was anger, it was played out for days under the coverlet of routine. If there was sadness it was accepted as a judgment, a note come due, nothing to whine about. Here was a man, though, who played out his emotions at the surface on the broad screen of face and body. He cried unashamedly, talked intemperately, opened the doors to his thoughts until the hinges creaked. She saw him fight his fear and compose himself. "Jillian, this does sound like one of Ned's bad jokes. I swear I wish it were. But here I am in the middle of a spy thriller. Salt: Schlamozzle from Nat Geo. Great word, 'schlamozzle.'"

She smiled, taking one of his hands again. "What's it mean?"

"Boris told me about it. A man who walks into a restaurant in a fog, looking for a friend perhaps, and backs into a waiter, who tips his tray of four orders onto the lap of an oblivious diner, this guy is a *schlemiel*. A guy who, over and over, without doing anything to invite it but for some cosmic offense in the past, gets trays for four dumped in his lap, along with cans of paint and peeing babies and leaking coffee cups, this one is a *schlamozzle*. The yin and yang of disaster. Oliver Hardy was your best-known schlamozzle. Charlie Salt is also a champion."

She laughed, and saw how a little laughter fueled him, powered his curve up.

"I do a layout for 'Star Wars,' trays for four drop out of low earth orbit onto my lap, radius of probable error, zero. I shouldn't laugh but it's all I can do. It's a damned Laurel and Hardy disaster without the loopy music. And then the dead guys. But they were trying to kill me for doing my goddamned job too well. I keep telling myself that. And then Murray. I'm still hoping he's okay. I'm very fond of Sparky."

She realized now why she had the desire to comfort him: she had watched him flash those emotions for years, finding them both fascinating and disturbing, too theatrical, too fulsome, too everything. But they were real.

"How about a drink?" she said. "There's a bottle in Ned Crocker's desk. Several."

"Good. Let me make this call about the kids. Can you drive me and the kids to National Airport in an hour or so? Am I getting in your hair, screwing up your plans? You have a big date tonight?"

She shook her head. "We'll get the kids. My car's in the garage. You have two kids, right? Who's watching them now?"

"I've got Mike and Sarah, twelve and sixteen. As for baby-sitters, nothing but the best for my guys: the KGB is watching them." He shook his head with an ironic smile, as if he'd dumped a bowl of cereal in his lap or gotten involved in international intrigue. "Look at this," he said, pulling out the automatic. "Heat."

"You're the least likely person to carry a pistol I've ever seen, Charlie Salt. You know how to use that?"

"I'm from a rural family. I can hit a groundhog sure as you're born, but I'm not sure I can shoot a man. Then again . . ."

"The man you—Did you shoot him?"

Charlie shook his head and put his eyes on some colored pencils: Not now.

"Okay. Make your call."

He made a call to Bath, Maine. She watched his face, saw it cycle through six emotions. When *Geographic* photographers got around to talking real stuff, late at night and drunk, or in the dark phases of their divorces, or when one of their own went down in a helicopter—when the truth mattered—they talked about distance. It was a common theme for people who lived behind polished lenses, the distance between them and life. To shoot a story, you walked in on people's lives, cut into their routines, and started taking thin slices of their existence, a five-hundredth of a second or a sixtieth. You needed a mask to make the intrusion plausible. For some, it was high spirits and jokes. Some used a counterfeit shyness. Some feigned clumsiness. The mask distanced you, made your invasion less painful, and when you found sickness and tragedy, the mask insulated you. It was a professional necessity that served you in the field and killed your marriage, strained your love life, compromised your friendships, and left you separate.

Charlie Salt had nothing between himself and life. It was an up-close life that burned him and bit him and froze him. He lived it close without the aid of a net. She admired his courage. She had once thought that a silent, strong woman could never have respect for an erratic man who cried and giggled. She wondered. She looked at him with a new affection and said, "Let's get the drink."

Ned Crocker was in his office. He always was, it seemed, late or early. He received Jillian appreciatively. She was wearing a black denim mini over blacker tights and an oversize coral blouse. Her dark hair was cut short and buzzed on top, shaggy and longer along her neck in back. A heavy gold bracelet emphasized her hands and forearms, and two bits of gold were half hidden in the dark hair around her ears. It was a look that would have been too severe for a European face. Her face, though, was softer, with high, rounded cheekbones and full lips. Her skin was the texture of very fine, very light lambskin leather, the color of terra cotta in the sun. She knew how she looked and how she affected men, and it was slightly annoying to her that Charlie was not responding to signals. She would not hit him over the head with it, goddammit.

But Ned was appreciative and alert to all the signals. He envied Charlie. Even at seventy-two, his fires were not out. "Jillian, my dear, and Charles, how delightful of you both to interrupt this dreary passage of words I'm pulling behind me. Welcome, my dears. Come, now, I know it's not in the current rulebook, but let us flaunt foolish fashion for friendships. Let me offer you a little something."

"A little something would be most welcome, guru."

"Charlie needs a stiff little something, Ned," she said. "But I'm the designated driver, and I'll have a small splash of your beautiful sherry, if I may."

"Then for Charles the Explainer, a dram of unblended Scotch. And for the lovely Jillian, a smooth bit of Jerez." He said it with the throaty *H* at the beginning and the lisp at the end, in the style of Madrid. Handing it to her, he gave her flowery compliments in his beautiful Castillian Spanish. She replied in her flatter southwestern Spanish that he was altogether too kind and should keep such compliments for fast horses or women of high birth. Charlie, who did not speak Spanish, drank his scotch, savored the smoky taste, and looked at the things on Ned's walls. It was very good scotch: he could feel it warm outward.

"But here we are conversing in a heathen tongue and shutting Charles out. I am a selfish man to embrace this extraordinary woman in the tongue of my adopted language." The sexual subtext was not lost on any of them: one admired Ned for the subtlety of his passes and hoped to emulate him. "Charles, you look disturbed this evening."

Charlie nodded. "You know I told you about a situation? I'm finding how rough they can be. They tried to kill me today."

"Good Lord, man. Kill you? Charlie, you must do something immediately. Speak to the intelligence oversight committee, to the FBI, to someone."

"It's gone a little beyond that. I'm involved in a way that requires . . ."

Charlie faltered, and Ned suggested, "As the Fat Man said, 'nice judgment'?"

"Just so."

"What can I do?"

"This is just fine for now." He held up the glass. "Not much anyone can do for a while, Ned."

"And your children?"

"Jillian's helping me get them out of town right now." He glanced at his watch and finished his drink with a grimace and a smile. "Hoo boy, good stuff."

"Anytime, my boy. And anything at my disposal is, you know, yours."

"Thanks, Ned."

Coming up out of the garage level, she handled her white BMW with skill, pushed it and used the gears well. He looked across at her face, grave with the concentration of driving in Washington, a city of lapsed learner's permits. The touch of scotch was warm in him, and he was going to say something common, pleasant, like "Thank you for the trouble, Jillian," or "Good of you to drive me home," but the gray-haired man lying on the back of the blue whale interfered.

So she said something, probably inappropriate. "How did your wife die, Charlie?"

"Drunk driver."

"How long ago?"

There was a longer pause this time. "Four years, two months, couple of weeks."

She nodded. "Miss her?"

"No."

She got the message but refused delivery. "I hear she was a nice lady."

He nodded. Kim had been a good city driver and he liked to be driven by her. He would watch the shops and the people as they came back from a show or dinner. He and Kim would talk, kiss at stoplights until the car behind beeped, hold hands between shifts. When he was puckish, he would reach across and stroke one breast and she would tell him that he was naughty, very naughty. He would nod, guilty as charged.

They were turning onto Thirty-fourth at the Naval Observator. Jillian was downshifting. Charlie realized that, before the shift, he had been holding Jillian's hand for two miles. She shifted up again and, strangely, took his hand in hers this time. She had very strong hands.

He thought about coming up the alley again, but it just wasn't his style. He and Jillian walked up to his front door.

Nikolai immediately hugged him. "Little brother, I was worried extremely." Petrov smiled in the background and shook his finger at Charlie, glancing at Jillian. Jillian caught the message, began to bristle, and found she was not at all unhappy about it. "What has happened, Charlie?"

"The Volvo died. Just like that. I drove down through Rock Creek Park and it started to sound rough, but it stopped by the Natural History Museum. A guy stopped behind me. I was frightened, so I went in. I didn't want to wander along the street with these guys after me and no Russian calvary." Petrov glanced at Jillian, but Nikolai's expression didn't change from its genial concern. *I'm glad you're my friends*, Charlie thought, *because I would not want you against me*. "Jillian is *Geographic*. She's helping," he explained.

"Good. Lovely to meet you, Jillian. You are photographer

with exhibit I send to Moscva only in last June, yes?"

She nodded and managed a smile. Charlie suddenly realized that he hadn't really explained the Soviet connection. Things had moved too fast; yesterday seemed like last week, life in the Cuisinart. "Jillian, Nikolai is one of my best friends. He and our friend Petrov Kruskin have been protecting me. Petrov saved my life yesterday."

"The Russian killed them, one, two." That *one*, she thought, and looked at him with her shooter's eyes. *Yes, he could.*

"But Charlie, what happened after Volvo stopped?"

"The man followed me into the Museum. I got up into the upper floor, which was closed. He had a gun. I waited for him, and I killed him." Charlie was idly tracing the pattern of the Persian rug with his eyes, his voice was someone else's.

"With the Walther?" Petrov asked. "With the gun I gave you?"

"No. I was afraid of the noise. I killed him with a flint-tipped spear. He's lying on the back of the blue whale."

Petrov and Nikolai looked at each other, eyebrows raised, and Nikolai went on. "Any interference? Any fuss from guards? No one sees you?"

"I don't think so."

"Tell you what, Charlie, when I have this small dacha, you come visit and lecture at KGB academy, yes? Good amateur work, especially spear. Seldom used in intelligence work now."

Petrov laughed, got up, and checked the windows, the back door. Jillian heard him put on the kettle, a domestic sound.

"Back to basic road, dear Charlie," Nikolai continued. "Mike is having trouble with math, and I am helpless at explaining. Petrov, however, is engineer, fixed him up."

"He is a bright boy," called Petrov. "He needs special classes to bring this out."

"Okay," Nikolai went on. "Sarah is on phone most of evening so far. I am told this is homework, doing it on the phone. I am willing this evening to be deceived, but I take it you are not every evening. I have taken liberty of asking them to put together some clothes, warm, for a trip. 'Where are we going?' Up to Charlie, I say. A little avoiding, so she does not say everything on phone, you see. They have had something to eat. A cheese omelet, very simple. They are ready and we are ready. Flight time is near. Petrov will follow you in another car and return with you. Will stay here tonight. I will be gone when you return but will see you tomorrow. Children will be safe. You will be safe. Work can proceed on story, yes?"

"Yes." Jillian questioned him with one bland look, and he replied with another, that said: On the way back from the airport, I'll explain everything. She concurred. *Odd*, he thought, *to talk without words again.*

But then Sarah came down with her bag, and Charlie realized that he had been talking without words all along. It was odd only in that Jillian was a grown woman. Sarah put her bag down confrontationally, square in the hall traffic pattern. This gesture said, Okay, I'm going nowhere until I'm told what's going on. She glanced back to Petrov making tea in the kitchen, and smiled a little too sweetly at Nikolai and looked at Charlie as one looks at a dishonest butcher— Well? Russians suddenly invade *my* house (the emphasis in this unspoken communication was on *her* space, *her* life), and you go mental on me. Here is my bag. I'm going this far for you, but no farther until I'm told.

Charlie looked at her thoughtfully, and nodded slightly; You're right, you've been invaded, you need some explanation. I will satisfy you.

Then Sarah looked at Jillian, blatantly appraisingly: Are you good enough to be here with this man? He is my father, but he is also my man. She looked at her face and up and down her, stopping just short of walking around her as she would in a furniture store.

Wrong again, Charlie, we've got two grown women here. Should I duck or get between with a pail of cold water? "Jillian Ansara, I'd like you to meet my oldest, brightest, and most beautiful daughter, Sarah. Sarah, this is Jillian, a photographer for the magazine."

There was a moment of danger. If Petrov had been in the hall, he would have had his hand near the little automatic. Sarah's face did not change: Goddammit. My house invaded, and now this bimbo. Good-looking, good dresser, expensive taste, bad timing.

Jillian cocked her head one centimeter and matched the silence, raised it and called, Hello, little girl, I am here on a woman's business, and some of it has to do with this frazzled man. Here's my deal: no mothering, no pink frilly frocks, you can be my friend if you know how to do that without getting in the way. I am a heavy, and you can learn something.

"I have two of your photographs on my wall. The women in Nepal. I think they're awesome. It's like you made me know the women. That's neat." Capitulation to her, not to Charlie.

"Do you take photography at school?"

"Yes. I'm pretty bad."

"No, she isn't," Charlie dared.

"I'd like to see some of your prints."

Good Lord, Charlie thought, this is serious business. He knew this was a major concession from a heavy cruiser to an escort destroyer. The density of this debate without words was tiring him out. He did what he could, given the circumstances: he bawled for Mike.

"Goddammit, Mike! I spend half my damned life by this front door waiting for you to zip up your damned fly and get down here, and when you get her you'll have forgotten half of what you need, you worthless street urchin."

A distant tumbling sound, louder, followed by Mike and a thickly packed bag.

"Okay, Dad. All ready."

After Mike had gone back for his toothbrush, hairbrush, extra underwear, slippers, book-report book, and nightshirt, they were in Jillian's car heading down Rock Creek Park, Petrov's car behind them.

"Dad?" Sarah asked.

"Yeah, Sadie?"

"Dad?" No need for clarification beyond a glance at Jillian: Is she all right with this?

"Okay, kid," Charlie said. "Mike, you listen up too." Mike's reaction to stress was cocooning, spinning a private web of inturning trivialities around and around until he seemed to be humming to himself in the corner of a car but was hiding somewhere deep. "This is the way it goes, the short version so far. Some guys at the Pentagon are worried about a layout I put together for a magazine story. Nikolai thinks they're running a secret project that no one else knows about, and they don't want attention focused on one of the weapons. They might want to stop me from trying to publish the thing. They might even want to hurt me. Doubtful, but there it is." Jillian looked at him briefly. He went on, "Nikolai and his friend Petrov, who is a specialist at protecting people, found out about the layout when Nick came to dinner with Allen and Marjorie . . . when was it, last week? That's about it."

"Where are we going?" Mike asked.

"You're going to stay with John Carter in Maine. He says you can help bring the boats up out of the water."

"Can I drive them?"

"I have no doubt that you'll get a turn at the wheel."

"Maine. In the fall. Boring. Everyone there is a hundred and five. God." Sarah did not want to leave her father.

"Except the kids at the Apprentice Shop. You'll be staying right next door."

She smiled. *She's growing up too fast,* Charlie thought.

The flight left. The kids had gum, a copy of *Elle*, an Almond Joy. Charlie and Jillian watched the plane through the big window gone black with night, seeing mostly their reflections but then the 727 hurtling past in the lights, rotating and climbing away from the smallest, most convenient, most dangerous airport in any American big city. Charlie lingered, saw Petrov for a moment behind him, milling in the crowd, and looked at Jillian's reflection in the glass. It was a good face that acted its age and kept its youth. It was a good neck. He noticed, probably not for the first time but certainly for the first time up close, that she had a wonderful body. Fine breasts, narrow waist, generous hips, good legs. When he looked back to her face, she was watching him inventory her, pursing her lips in a mocking smile: *Charlie, you dog.* He gave her a present he hadn't given away in years, a shit-eating grin.

On the way back, they talked about the story, about the Russians, about Murray, about the problems he would have selling the layout to Stone. They talked about her shoot, then about her work in general and how she worked with Gabe and with the Society. She talked about what she wanted to do.

"There's a lot I want to see, Charlie. I've been around a lot but there's more. I have a lot of places to go. I can't get tied down."

"Absolutely. You're a shooter, Jills. Shooters move. Nature of the beast." *Don't patronize me, Ansara. I'm not applying for the goddamned position.*

"Clive's not the only one who can do South America, you know. I haven't even scratched the surface of what I want do with the women of the Andes."

"Ought to be a great story. And you ought to write it."

"I'm a shooter."

"So was Abercrombie, basically a shooter. Now he writes, too. It's communication, pictures on the eye, on the tongue. Same difference."

"You think I could write?"

"I do."

"There's so much to do."

"A lot."

"Don't get sad, Charlie."

"Was I getting sad? Not me. No, I was thinking of something else, missing the guys. I'm used to them." He was thinking of Jillian, and of Kim, whom he would love right up to the time they lowered the Society's blue and green and brown flag for him. They all go. Rock Creek Park at night, a texture passing and a streaming pearl necklace of headlights. He knew tonight that Sarah was a young woman and she would go soon. Kim had gone, unfairly and untimely. This sweet woman, Jillian, had stepped into his life unbidden, attracted by God knows what, by some warmth she needed, and she would take the warmth and share the hearth and the laughter for a time, and she would be on her way too. Off for the world.

Charlie Salt felt old and knew how difficult it was to live with his intensity, how it ate up the oxygen around him. He knew the intensity was the reason his friends loved him, and it was also the reason Jillian or anyone else would go. Not South America, not more rolls of film, just a lack of oxygen. He faced the fact that Kim had been thinking about leaving too.

Have I changed since then? The texture of Rock Creek Park had not changed. Maybe he had. But the burning fuse of his drive, he knew, would always be spitting and consuming the air in him.

$$\triangledown$$

Chapter 12

CHARLIE SALT WAS DREAMING in color. Kim came to him, and everything was right. She was not backing away from him, wanting space. He was giving space without knowing it. It was easy in the dream. They walked in the rain the played against the porch roof outside his window, outside his dream. They loved the rain. It would be simple: she would go back to school; he would fly to her on weekends . . .

Gray and light gray, the streetlight cast shadows of the window mullions against the dresser, cast shadows of the dresser against the door, of the door against the wall. A dark gray oblong beside the bathroom door was her picture. He had wanted to live a good life of explaining the world and die, very hold, holding her hands. He saw the hands inside his color-corrected head, compact and graceful, fitting together like Japanese packaging, the fingers slightly blunt like her toes but seemly, right for her rare gestures. She was not a demonstrative woman. He wished her back with all his guilt and all his lost saints and risked his own unique hell by calling on a God that evaporates before science writers like desert mirages. *Same deal as I'd make with the gray-haired man: I'll be good forever, never do anything wrong. I won't drink any more beer.*

This was so ridiculous that Charlie and Kim, if she was anywhere nearby, snickered silently at Charlie Salt passing up a frosted Sapporo.

He grieved with every change in the weather, with every sauce he made on the stove, with every time he changed his sheets. He was a faithful man in his unusual way. It was why she loved him and why she had wanted to leave him.

He was awake because someone had flushed the toilet and there was a light under the door. Mike. No, Mike and Sarah were in Bath; the call had come. Petrov. He was downstairs, padding around, napping in dark corners. Yes, Jillian, who stayed in the guest room at Petrov's suggestion. It would be good to see her in the morning. The light went out, and Charlie's door opened.

She stepped around the door and looked at the bed, adjusting her eyes to the dark again. "Is there a lock?" she asked.

Charlie nodded, realized she couldn't see him, and said, "Yes. Shoulder high."

She closed the door gently and slid the bolt to. She did not say anything else but took off Mike's T-shirt and dropped it at the foot of the bed. She stood there in black panties, letting Charlie see the streetlight cast the shadows of her breasts across her body. Or perhaps she was thinking about something else. The effect confused him.

She slipped into the bed, pulling the blankets around her shoulders like a broad cape as she crouched above Charlie, knees on either side of his hips. He could see her eyes for a moment; they watched him for a sign of something and did not find it. They were almost angry. She leaned forward and began to kiss the side of his neck where the pulse was. The tips of her breasts touched his chest. As she moved up and over, kissing his high brow, under which all the foolishness resided, her nipples grew harder and moved against him. she kissed his left ear now, delicately, playing with the flange of stiff flesh at the edge with her pointed tongue. Charlie put his hands on her hips and felt them stir like slow waves. He stroked the skin and flesh of her hips, and the waves grew. She kissed his mouth now, hungry. He was beginning to explore; she was feasting. It was unfamiliar to Charlie, a woman who pursued him. He reached up and under, as he lay on his back, for her breasts as they swung with fleshy slowness, still brushing him. He grasped them, hard, and she left his mouth part of an inch and sighed, saying without words, Yes, that, do that.

It was not enough for her. She moved up and took her right breast in her hand. "Take that," she hissed softly, and fed it to Charlie's mouth. She shuddered. "Bite," she ordered, and he bit as tentatively as a dynamiter bites a cap. It was enough; she shuddered harder.

It was not enough. She moved up farther and opened her lower lips to him. Charlie was beginning to feast, tasting her, looking up past her thighs and belly to the architecture of her breasts and the structure of her jaw as it worked, sighing and breathing. And then, as Charlie reached around from her buttocks up to her breasts and grasped them again, she put her hands over his and made a harsh, dying sound of pain and release, pushing her mound against his mouth: All of it now, do it all now. And he did, and she arrived.

She kneeled above him, stiff for a moment, and collapsed beside him. He was not sure, but felt what might have been tears. He held her. But she was not done.

In his fascination with her climax, he had forgotten his own. He was wilted but still caring. She kissed down toward him and took him in her mouth. From his head on the pillow it seemed like a long way to his cock, but reports were good.

She did things that felt good, short fluttering things and long pulling things and all the wet things. Charlie, who was very oral, respected her talent. He wanted her to finish him in her mouth, but he was not the conductor here. She pivoted around and took him in her hand and used him against her like a smooth stick, like an erotic fruit. Then he was in her and she was melting around him, and she did all the work. Except that he made her breasts swing even more with his hands, and except taking her face harshly just before he arrived and kissing her deeply, desperately, bucking up into her and almost going crazy with confusion and relief and pleasure and guilt. He cried. She held him, kneeling with his seed and his flesh still in her, holding his head to her strong shoulders.

She did not know why he was so upset but it was not a problem for her to feel this way about Charlie. What way? *Hush*, she said to herself. "Hush," she said to Charlie, and held him.

"Quiet, you guys. I can't hear myself think. Okay, you say that this is a laser mounted in a B-52 that can zap missiles?"

Jillian took over from Gabe, explaining the second spread of the layout. The layout room was filled. Stone, Gabe, Jillian, Ballisterio, Charlie, plus the associate editors and the science editor. This was the working layout session, the proof of concept that showed Stone a layout was possible. "Accuracy is controlled by the same radar used in F-14s. The weapon itself is a powerful CO_2 laser that has a range of several miles. It's not the ultimate shield weapon that everyone's projected but it's a demonstration that it can be done."

"Have we got pictures of what it does?" Stone asked.

"Next spread," Gabe replied.

Charlie's explanation of orbital principles had been moved back to make room for the explosion of a drone and the beginning of text. It was a good decision.

"I don't know that we need three columns for a puff of smoke and some debris here," Stone said. "Bob, why don't you see if you can work up the turn with a flatter proportion, like this. . . ." He took a blank layout sheet and drew shapes on it. John Wheeler Stone had come up to be the editor through his layout department. It was still his, and he had the proportions in his head. "Have an explanation down here and an inset of the explosions over here. That's all we need, really. You see one explosion, you've seen them all."

Gabe Cooper shrugged at Jillian behind Stone's back. To get the shot, she had spent days in the back seat of a T-38 with a long lens, flying close to the laser path. The sad thing was that Stone was usually right.

"Okay, Charlie. What are you trying to put over on me now?" Stone looked at Salt in mock dismay. He wanted to encourage him; his explanations were good ones, but he had to be controlled. Charlie had a tendency to try to explain how the world fit together in two pages. Stone loved enthusiasm. He also knew how harshly he had to control his own enthusiasm, so he came down on Charlie's regularly.

"Simple stuff, John. The Star Wars constellation of surveillance, communication, and deterrence satellites move in ways that are predetermined by orbital mechanics. If they use their hydrazine thrusters to speed up, they must gain altitude. If they brake, they slow down and they lose altitude. But when they lose altitude, there is more energy available. It has to do with Kepler's Law. . . ."

"Spare me. Let me live in ignorance of something, okay?"

"Okay, it loses altitude, gains energy, speeds up, and gains altitude. Life is funny in orbit."

"Hold it." Sean McCorley, an associate editor, saw a paradox, one of those leaks in sense he and his people—the writers, legend writers, researchers and issue editors that made up his bailiwick—would plug. "You're saying that this little fellah brakes, slows down, loses altitude, and because of that he speeds up and gains altitude?"

Charlie nodded, then shrugged. "That's why we need a page of explanation. All these garbage cans . . ."

Jillian cleared her throat. If Stone noticed he said nothing.

". . . all these jewellike satellites are in constant relative motion. They swing around the earth in elliptical orbits, and within the discipline of their orbit they maintain a relative motion. To target a missile coming downrange, you must know the exact location of the battle-station satellite, within centimeters. Hunter-killer satellites sent up against battle stations rendezvous with their prey using the same complex orbital mechanics. Navigation satellites, communication satellites function . . ."

"You've convinced me," Stone said.

"They all respond to laws quantified by Newton and . . ."

"Stop. I give up. Do it," Stone said. "Let's move on. I've got a lunch." Stone watched Jillian shift past Charlie, saw him touch her waist as she passed him. *Curious pairing*, he thought. His antennae were always deployed for international politics or musky doings. He gave it a few moments of thought as he gazed at the next spread and knew that it would not go well for Charlie. She was a shooter, and she was on the move. He was a father; his place was to make stability, here on the eighth floor and at home. They were pretty together, though. *I hope it's worth it, Charlie*, he said to himself, and then gave himself over to Jillian's shoot.

"What have we got here? Looks like a cat's cradle."

"Close," Charlie said. "This is Dauphain. We've

scrounged and researched and put together the cutting edge in 'Star Wars' technology. This is a nuclear-pumped X-ray laser missile. Not a satellite. It's called a pop-up because it's shot up from a submarine on a missile launcher before it works. Hostile missiles, in red . . ." Charlie explained his new rendering of the layout for two and a half minutes, moving slowly and simply through the principles.

"This is fascinating," the science editor said. "How did you get all this detail? Good stuff, Charlie."

Bob Ballisterio nodded.

Gabe, the picture editor, said, "It extends our whole coverage of the subject."

Stone stood in front of the page. He shook his head. "It's outside the SDI concept. It's like artillery. It's not a battle station in orbit. No, it's just not part of the story."

Charlie's stomach ran into his bowels. "We have a chance here to show what's not in the book yet."

"It can't be in the book. Look, deploying nuclear weapons in space is against the 1972 treaty limiting antiballistic missiles. They're not going to put this on a missile submarine.

"They are if it's already developed, if it's ready, if the technology is in place. It's the technological imperative: If they can, they will."

"Do you have any reason to think someone is actually developing it?"

"We think they are. We're running it down."

"Who have you got researching it?" Stone asked.

"Murray Hofnung was . . ."

"Where in hell *is* Hofnung?"

"We've got Helen on it, now."

"Doesn't matter," Stone said. "It doesn't fit."

"It's part of the whole concept."

Stone looked at the spread. Something bothered him about it, and something bothered him about the way Charlie was arguing for it. "Hang it up, Charlie. Let's move on."

"Think about it. I'll get more information, and you can see if it fits for you."

"Okay, goddammit. Now, can we move along, for Christ's sake?" A rare burst of anger in the layout room.

Half an hour later, Stone was talking to Gabe and Jillian about holes in the coverage. Charlie walked to his office wanting badly to sit down. Carlton Deauville was waiting, sitting at Charlie's conference table with his hat on, reading a copy of the magazine.

Charlie stood by the door until Deauville looked up, and then he knew he should close the door.

"Inspector Deauville."

"Mr. Salt. You want to sit down, Mr. Salt?"

"I think I'll stand right here, if you don't mind. What can I do for you?"

"Are you Mr. Murray Hofnung's immediate superior?"
Shit. "I am."

"Does Mr. Hofnung reside at 4235 Tunlaw Road?"

"I believe so, Inspector." The day outside was cloudy; it could rain. Birds sat on the cornices of the M Street building across from Charlie's window. *Come on, Murray, don't leave me with this.*

"I'm sorry to have to tell you that our investigations indicate that Mr. Hofnung died sometime last Thursday. We found the body in his apartment, and we're completing forensic workups and dental records. You want to sit down now?"

"No." The birds weren't going anywhere. They nodded to one another and walked along the cornice. *They live on the edge easily*, he thought, *but falling well is their business.*

"I have to ask you some questions. Not going to be

pleasant. Don't want you to get offended, take it personal, nothing like that. You can do that?"

"I don't know. I'm personally involved in this. It will be hard not to take some of it personally."

"We'll try. Up to you." He reached inside his camel-hair jacket and brought out a notebook and a ballpoint pen. "You don't have to answer any of my questions, Mr. Salt. You can have an attorney present, you know."

"You sound like I'm under suspicion, Inspector."

"You understand that you answer only what you want to answer, right? Also that I'm requesting your help with this investigation, right? Good. Yes, there are a couple of things that I'd like you to clear up. Like how did you know Hofnung was in trouble the day he disappeared?"

Charlie looked at him. *Life is complicated in orbit, all right. Be careful.*

"He's a reliable guy."

"More than that, Mr. Salt."

"It boils down to this: I'm involved in some sensitive work. I'm pretty sure that my office was searched on the night that our guard was killed. . . ."

"Mr. Wheeler."

"Corporal Wheeler, yes. I believe Corporal Wheeler's death had something to do with the search, which had to do with the sensitive nature of the work. The next day, Murray was to research the story and he didn't come in after that. It was an assumption on my part."

"Whenever someone makes an assumption like that, whenever the assumption comes true, I've got to know more. This doesn't come out right for me, not at all. Makes me nervous, Mr. Salt. Hofnung was found in his apartment in pretty bad shape. Dead four or five days in a really hot apartment, both of them."

"Both of them?"

Deauville had waited for Charlie's reaction to the first piece of information. Satisfactory. Now the second.

"Yeah. Hofnung and his fancy boy. Hooker from P Street Beach named Judd Penn. Know him?"

Charlie caught the implication. "No. I doubt that Murray knew him, either."

"Murray not gay?"

"No."

"Tough thing to know for sure, Mr. Salt."

"Probably. I have a lot of respect—"

"Had."

". . . had a lot of respect for Murray. If he were gay, it wouldn't be an issue to hide. He might not wave it, but he wouldn't hide it. No."

"We find him in bed with a gay hooker. We also find a quantity of uncut cocaine beside the bed. Cause of death: drug overdose."

"No."

"No again, Mr. Salt. This Hofnung was one righteous puppy."

"He couldn't do drugs at all. He had a fear of drugs, even aspirin."

"Where do you come into all of this, Mr. Salt? You knew he was gone, you knew he was missing. You are certain about something you won't talk about. What is it?"

"Murray Hofnung was killed. Murdered. Someone in the intelligence community killed him and planted him in his apartment with a hooker and cocaine to discredit him."

"It certainly does that."

"It's a goddamned shame. I liked Murray."

"How much, Mr. Salt?"

"Fuck you, Inspector. Take your notebook and your hat

and get the fuck out of my office."

"Sorry, Mr. Salt. I ask questions like that because the way
you answer it makes a lot more information than what you
answer. I apologize. Can we go on? What intelligence organization? DIA, CIA, Army Intelligence, Naval Intelligence?
Lot of spooks around this District."

"I don't know."

"How do you know they did it at all?"

"Because they tried to kill me."

"How?"

Careful. "They watched my house. One of them tried to
kill me when I was running."

"You know, Mr. Salt, I watch all the houses on my street,
just out of curiosity, you know, but I'm not CIA. Just
occasionally nosy, and some folks get thinking, you know,
about their 'sensitive work' and imagine all kinds of folks
are snooping in on them. This running murder attempt? It
wouldn't have been down at the canal, would it?"

"No."

"That's inconvenient. Now, I could tie that into something real, but this doesn't make sense to me yet. You got
anything else in the spook line, Mr. Salt?"

"You're an insulting son of a bitch, Inspector."

"Well, now, that's the work, you know? We probing
around old dead bodies lying in hot apartments four and five
days, we jiving with executive types who won't tell what they
know and call us sons of bitches, we get naturally pissy. But
we keep plenty of control and don't slam them up against
their office walls. Even though it might ought to be the best
thing for them, get stuff out in the open and let someone
help whose job it is. But you play it your way, Mr. Salt. This
come under freedom of the press? Something like that, I
suppose. So you got my card and you can call me if you think

of anything you want to tell me. And when I go over to see my mother Sunday lunchtime, I'm going to tell on you, that you said she's a bitch, and that lady may come over and kick your whitebread ass. She's a feisty old lady. Got less control than me."

"Hey, Deauville. Tell your mama I shouldn't say bad things about her. Tell her I get scared and real careful."

"Yeah. Don't get so careful you get yourself hurt, Mr. Salt."

"You believe me, don't you?"

"Hell. It doesn't matter. Can't act on it. Still not enough. Got some doubts about the whole look of the damn thing, though. You sure you can't tell me more?"

"I'm not holding back stuff that would help."

"Best I be the judge of that."

"Sorry. I've got to be careful. I could get burned real bad."

"Mmm." Deauville dipped his hat brim and thought a moment while he put away his notebook and pen. He nodded his head, got up, and walked out. As he turned the corner, he said, "Call," without looking back or revealing his eyes.

I've got to get a hat like that, Charlie thought.

$$\triangledown$$

Chapter 13

Harold Dorffer came scuttling down the corridor clutching a sheaf of sketches. A broad, white smile emerged from his gray beard and made him resemble Santa Claus, if Santa wore bow ties and was the CEO of a corporate Christmas conglomerate instead of a hardworking saint. He had a kind word for everyone along the hall, the consummate politician, and his endearingly pudgy fingers were twiddling, feeling for all the pies they were in. He was having fun. After twenty-eight years of carrying the graphics of the Society into new territory, he felt he deserved fun. Charlie lay in wait. He was going to kill him.

"Harold! Where were you when I needed you? The 'Star Wars' layout sessions went down this morning. I could have used some backup. I got my second spread shot right down. We need that spread."

"Was that this morning? Whoa, it's just been a shit storm. I had so many meetings this morning. We had a great time. I met with the advertising people on the new poster campaign. . . ."

Charlie made an awful noise that did not sound like it came from a primate.

"Went badly, huh?" Harold asked.

"The Stone hates the second spread, and I maintain it's an important part of the story. He says it isn't what he wants to say about 'Star Wars'. But it's cutting-edge stuff. We dug it up just like we dug up the Stealth bomber."

Dorffer shook his head. There were battles he would not fight anymore; he had fought enough. "It's his magazine."

"It's *our* magazine."

Dorffer gave him a weak, fuzzy smile.

It tweaked Charlie's conscience. "Harold. Come on into your office and sit down. I've got something to tell you."

Dispensing good cheer, Harold swept on down the corridor and into his office with Charlie in his wake. The phone was ringing.

"Don't get the phone, Harold. Let it roll over. This is important."

Harold picked it up. "Harold Dorffer. Hello, May! Yes, that was lovely. We must do it more often. Of course I can help . . ." Harold held up one twiddling finger as he always did: Just one minute, be off in one minute only.

"Murray Hofnung is dead," Charlie said in a normal tone. Harold heard.

"May . . . yes, May, something's just come up here. How about I have Christy call you, and we'll set up some lunch. Or something. Soon." His smile had sunk into his beard, and his eyes looked old instead of crinkly and fun. He hung up without saying good-bye.

Charlie closed the door.

"Dead? Are you sure? Why are you talking to me about spreads if Murray is dead?"

"Inspector Carlton Deauville of the D.C. homicide division was just here. There's more. It's not good."

"Good Lord. Murray?"

"I know. There's more."

Harold looked up, frightened behind the beard.

"He was murdered."

Harold got up as if he had just been called to a meeting in Stone's office. He walked around his desk and returned to his chair. He sat down. "How?"

"It ties in with this layout and with Corporal Wheeler's death. I guess that's why I lump them in together."

"That's not so. Stop being ridiculous." Harold was frightened, all right.

Charlie tried to tell him about the layout. He did not tell him about the Soviets, or about the men on the towpath, or about the man on the whale's back, but he tried to get his help. Harold had brought him to the *Geographic*, brought him into the family; Charlie would always be grateful, no matter how angry he was at Harold's abandonment of the department.

"We think it's an outlaw intelligence outfit. The only thing I can figure is that they've got financial connections with a prime contractor for the project. They want to quash the story, and they needed to discredit Murray. They planted him in a seedy scene that's going to hurt his family. I wish we could do something about it."

"No. You've got it mixed up. I don't even want to hear this foolishness. This is no time to make up things like this. I won't be part of it." He picked up the phone. "Will. Harold Dorffer. I've got some bad news."

It just wasn't in him. He had fought too many battles, had lost too many times. The regularity of defeat had beaten his spirit. Charlie felt sorry for his old friend, the man who had made him a part of the family. The old man had lost his manhood.

Even so, Charlie walked with Harold down the corridor to the elevator banks at the center of the floor and across to the

Seventeenth Street windows. The sky was even grayer, and only a few of the crows that lived on the roof of the building across the street were making sorties. They flew among the telecommunications dishes and the antennae like fugitive notes from a dirge. Harold and Charlie looked down. With rain coming, they were smaller four-by-six flags and not the big spinnaker cloth floaters. They saw the guard come out and watched the *Geographic* flag, blue and green and brown, lower away from them, down to the fourth floor.

Back in his office, Harold began to stuff his briefcase with the six or eight pounds of supplies that might be necessary on the way home. He put on his trench coat and stood looking at the shelves of *National Geographics*, an almost complete set from 1890 to this month's issue.

"Forget about this crazy stuff. You should maybe take some time off. Why don't you take your kids and go to the country for a week. You've got loads of leave time. You're getting the story fever. You'll see things more clearly once you've taken some time off." Harold feared craziness anywhere near him.

"I've got stories I have to do," Charlie reminded him, even though Harold should know. But Harold had lost interest and would never be the same.

Charlie put his arm around Harold's shoulder and gave him a hug, then watched him scuttle down the hall, eager for the Mayflower Hotel's gin.

Maybe Stone is right about the spread, Charlie thought, watching Dorffer go. He almost always was. Sometimes Charlie felt as though his job was merely to set up targets for the Stone's target practice.

Harold Dorffer turned the corner to the elevators.

Charlie felt his job, his life here, was a matter of honor. They were most of them samurai, skilled in their own disciplines, who had pledged themselves to a warlord. They could doubt the warlord's individual decisions, but their honor lay in carrying out his overall orders. It was easy to be impatient with perceived lapses of judgment, but no one could doubt the Stone's course for the magazine. It comforted Charlie to hang his honor on something larger. But Charlie now knew that he needed a backup plan. Where did that come in?

Charlie started to bring the current layout to a point where he could see everything and understand the black-and-white relationships. He sprayed it with workable fixative, coughed, and brought himself to a decision. He made a call across town and arranged for a backup. He had done a thing that might have shamed a samurai, made him a *ronin*, a warrior without a warlord, but he knew it was a thing a warlord would do.

Chapter 14

"GOOD NI-GHT," RUTH CALLED, singing it and giving the second word two syllables. She went to this trouble when it had been a long, complicated day. She was still putting on her coat. "Going on the Metro with me?"

"No, I'll stay and finish up this new layout."

"What about Mike and Sarah?"

"They're out of town, visiting friends."

"It's not a school holiday." Ruth knew his life as well as he did.

"Explain it later."

"I don't know what to think about Murray. I mean, really. We would sit out here and talk about just everything in the Society and everybody. I never knew anyone who wanted to know more. He wasn't with us for long, but my God, he was really . . . family, you know?"

"I know."

"You're broken up about it. That's understandable, but it's not your fault."

He hadn't told her about the layout yet. Repeating it over and over made it sound even less plausible than it did the first time. He nodded.

"Oh, but guess who's coming down the hall. Someone to

see our favorite art di-rec-tor."

Charlie looked out the door to see Jillian passing Printing and Engraving.

"Stop singing the last part of every sen-tence," he said, singing the last part. "Go home and have a drink with your Charlie and get la-id." He was getting into the singing. They would probably do it for days now.

"It's a wonderful idea on a rainy ni-ght. Hello, Jil-li-an."

"Have I walked into an opera?"

"A comic operetta. Ruth is about to do the soliloquy about how she's going to take advantage of her Charlie. Then I do the Mad Scene. It's great."

"It's true, he does a great Mad Scene. No one better. We-ll," she said, returning to singing, "I'd better get to the Met-ro. Then to Char-lie. You two have fu-un. Avoid embarrassment and don't forget to lock your do-or." Ruth hurried down the hall, waving behind her.

"How does she know I jumped your bones, Charlie? Do you tell her everything?"

"Come on in so I can lock my do-or. No, I didn't tell her. A person like me, it might as well be written on my forehead: 'Recently laid.' Special glow, sheepish grin, renewed interest in life. That stuff."

She turned away and examined a rack of colored pencils. "These are neat."

Oh, Christ, she's worried now. "Jillian. I liked being with you. But I heard you tell me you aren't available for long-term assignment. I'm not going broody on you, pal. I haven't picked out a silver pattern, okay?" *Ouch, wrong thing to say.*

She was still fascinated by the pencils. "I move around a lot. I don't know what my next assignment will be."

He could feel her ambivalence. She wanted to turn away from the colored pencils and walk out the door and be shut

of him. That was simplicity. She wanted to hold him and
be held and listen to him rattle on and be a part of his
schemes and warmth. That was complicated, but it was
also life.

He was ambivalent, too. Should he try to hold anyone
balanced so finely between wanting him and not wanting
him? Shouldn't he wait and choose someone who was for
him, for intensity, for a complication of life?

Hell, no. The best of them would always be wary of him.
They would always be independent women who had their
own intensity and objected to his, who had enough complication without his plans. He was older, and his hurts had
either made him wiser or more wary. Either way, he moved
more slowly and let more opportunities pass. He had pursued Kim every day of their life together. He had loved her,
wanted her, needed her, controlled her that much. If Kim
were here now, could he work it differently? But then, she
wasn't. Sitting in his office chair in the midst of rumors of
death, he realized that he knew things about Kim and about
himself he hadn't known before.

So what about the woman who was here, who was about
to leave his office? "Jillian. You've got a new assignment
right now? If so, bon voyage, catch you on the flip side. If
not, let's feel it out, see how it feels. No vine-covered cottage.
I don't need a mother for my children. I'm Mom. And I don't
need a mother for me. I need a good woman, though. You're
a dandy. You're worried about getting in too deep, too sticky
for a shooter with ambition?"

She nodded her head.

"Jillian. I've got a serious question for you along these
lines."

She turned with a set in her eyes, ready to explain her need
for autonomy.

"Jillian, would a blowjob be entirely out of the question here?"

She broke up. "Well, really, you know. I used to have this rule about every room in the house . . ."

They were laughing when Charlie's phone rang. "Salt," he answered. "Yes, hello. Okay, fine, thanks."

She was still laughing. "Look, everyone's gone. It's . . ." she looked at her watch, ". . . it's seven-thirty. It really isn't completely out of the question if your office hasn't been really anointed. Who was it, anyway?"

"Ah, the moment is past. It's Petrov and Nikolai on their way up. Guard called. 'Your friends have arrived.' " The smile stayed on Charlie's face, but the laughter died. "Nikolai wouldn't bring Petrov here. I'm supposed to call Petrov to be picked up."

She looked at him with her own laughter drying and caking in her throat.

"Let's get out of here."

He took her hand, and they ran across the south corridor as they heard the elevator ring its arrival in the middle of the floor.

They ran up the west corridor, past the layout rooms, as far as Printing and Engraving's west door. It was dark in the viewing rooms where the color-corrected lights were turned off for the night. Two men passed their narrow band of view as they stepped carefully down the east corridor. They both had guns with silencers.

She tapped his shoulder and held up her finger and thumb: Your gun?

He raised his hands and his eyes, and pointed apologetically at his office.

She managed to screw up her mouth at him: Nice work, James Bond.

He beckoned and pointed: We'll go along the west corridor out of here.

She shook her head. She leaned close to his ear and breathed, "I think someone passed behind us. Don't know who. Just saw a shadow. Could be wrong."

He leaned to her. "Good enough for me. Wait till these guys go into my office and run down past the elevators to the little elevator by Al's office?"

She nodded. Good.

He peeked out, just like in cowboys and Indians. He felt distinctly like an Indian, unless this was the Little Bighorn. He signaled to her, Come on, kid, and took her hand and they rushed up the corridor. Even as they were fleeing from death, Charlie realized that the gait with which they ran, trying to move swiftly but quietly, hoping there were no noisy dimes in the pockets, closely resembled a fast Groucho Marx walk. His mind was clear and working fast. He managed a look at the good woman beside him. Maybe that's life all around: we try to be graceful, and the best we can manage is ridiculous. They were almost at the turn in the corridor past the elevators. They made it.

But a slug bit at the wall just as they turned. "Shit!" Charlie hissed, and they abandoned Groucho for Jesse Owens.

The little elevator was a hydraulic: it would take ages to arrive. No possibility there. He pulled her into Jon Schnee-berger's office. It was dark and ominous, hung with South American memorabilia, feathers and arrows and bones and a skull. He pointed to the phone and tapped his finger on the air frantically: Call the guard. He looked around him for possibilities and found some slim hope hanging on the wall.

The two men from the Outfit split up, using hand signals. They were good at their work, and they were certain that dealing with a Soviet operative required their best. Especially after he had killed one of their most experienced operatives, Steve Burns. They listened, and were fairly sure of the office that Salt was in. One of them would move in slowly. They had found a Walther PP in Salt's briefcase, but this meant nothing. They would assume he had a gun. Their field captain was going over Salt's office for documents. One of the men held up a finger and moved toward the door.

He came around the door smoothly, low. His eyes did not immediately follow the jumbled pattern of the room, the colored feathers. He saw Jillian at the telephone and began to lay the revolver between her shoulder blades when feathers came leaping toward him. There was a swish and a hum, a slap and then a pain. He stumbled back into the light and looked at himself, decorated from the middle with a four-foot Orinoco arrow, fletched with beautiful macaw feathers, the shaft cut in patterns. He could see one inch of the five-inch head that anchored the shaft in him. He could not know, though he might presently guess, that it had been steeped in curare beside a tributary of the Amazon, and that the poison was still remarkably potent. A numbness was spreading through his middle with the pain, and breathing was becoming difficult. He put his gun on a counter and held the shaft carefully, deciding to sit down. He found one of the secretary's chairs and sat down slowly and died.

Charlie put down the wooden bow. He took a handful of little rubber bands that picture editors use to bind stacks of slides. Jillian was still punching the buttons. Nothing. The guard was gone in the front hall. He touched her shoulder and shook his head. Time to go, he mouthed, and pointed out the door. But first—he held up a hand—he would find out where the other one was.

He popped his head around the corner and back. A slug hit the metal door a moment later, making a loud slap.

Charlie nodded and pointed: He's south along the east corridor, waiting. More pointing: We go across the secretarial pool to the east corridor. Ready?

The second Outfit man prepared to move in, sparing a glance for his colleague, who did not look good. As he rose to slip against the wall, Salt's hand swung around the jamb and a black canister, hissing furiously, came tumbling through the air toward him. Where did he get that? He dived through the nearest door and covered his ears against the blast of a concussion grenade but heard Salt and the woman rush out of the office and across to the far corridor. He waited thirty seconds, but there was no blast. The hissing stopped. He looked out and picked up the canister, a can of Kleen Slide compressed air, cold from decompression, its trigger bound down with rubber bands.

He ran down the corridor and called to his field captain, "Hey! They're on the move, and they got Henderson."

The captain rushed up with his own gun drawn. "Dammit, Holzer. Which way?"

"Down the far stairwell."

They ran to the stairwell and could hear Charlie and Jillian running down toward the basement.

"They'll be going to the M Street building. Probably up to Photo. That's where her office is. Come on."

They took the elevator and saved time. As the doors opened in the basement, they heard Charlie and Jillian run off the linoleum of the long corridor under the courtyard to the carpet of the M Street elevators. Trotting along the corridor, they heard the ring of an elevator and a door close. Holzer looked at his captain, who shrugged as they trotted: We know where they're going.

The street seemed as dangerous as the compound. It was

foolish but it was home. Jillian was leading now, down the halls of the second floor toward her office, a lockable haven. Once again, Charlie had the feeling he was playing everyone else's game.

They passed custom photo equipment, and he skidded to a stop, holding her hand. Kristoff's Ball, a beautiful sphere of polished glass holding flashbulbs for broad underwater photos, gleamed from a cart. Behind them, the elevator announced the arrival of their guests.

He vaulted over the counter in his excitement and she slithered after him, frantic with fear and confusion: What are we doing here?

He touched the smooth surface of the Ball with all ten fingertips, letting it think for him. He whispered roughly to Jillian, "Rig it," and she understood. In a few seconds, she had fetched a large rechargeable from the battery locker and fastened one lead from the Ball to one of its terminals. Charlie opened the door to the corridor and wheeled the Ball into its opening, noticing a small complaint from one wheel of the car. *Stay open, Charlie, play your own game.* Charlie and Jillian retreated under the counter.

Holzer's heart was not in wet work. The man was a Soviet assassin, clearly, but hunting men—and women—in the city was not the open jungle hunting he could believe in. He had been a sixteen-cent killer in 'Nam, a sniper who infiltrated, waited, and did an assigned job with one sixteen-cent round of 30.06 ball ammunition. In Central America, he had tracked specific targets for days, weeks, and had disappeared them. That was different. It was an extension of his boyhood, hunting and poaching in the hills of Ohio. This was the *National Geographic*, for Christ's sake. He looked to his captain for guidance.

The captain signaled. We'll split up. I'll take the north

approach to her office, you go up the south side. Holzer nodded and tried to think of it as a drywalled jungle.

He passed, carefully, an open counter window marked "Custom Photo Equipment." Door on his right blocked by a strange device. Why is the door blocked? He looked behind him; his captain was on the far corridor already. He approached the gleaming ball, a piece of science fiction sculpture that drew the eye: a machined aluminum collar holding an optical glass hemisphere, big, with dozens of white bulbs within it. He touched the glass with his free hand, acknowledging an impulse it seemed to radiate.

Kristoff's Ball, named after the underwater innovator and photographer Emory Kristoff, was designed to illuminate areas of seafloor archaeology or feeding ground. It has an array of thirty #40 flashbulbs. Any three of these powerful bulbs would be sufficient to illuminate the entire facade of the Seventeenth Street building for a night shot with relatively slow film. It could pump almost a billion candlepower into the abyssal depths. Holzer gazed into it once more as he moved the cart, noticing that one wheel squeaked.

Charlie tapped Jillian's arm and covered his face with an arm. Jillian turned away and made the last connection. Kristoff's Ball illuminated the south side of the second floor, blackening the finish on the wooden door near it, singeing papers on the bulletin board, leaving a slight shadow-graph of the cart on the carpet. Holzer's scruples about urban wet work were suddenly academic. His shirt was burned, the skin on the backs of his hands and his face was blackened. His facial hair had disappeared, leaving a white powder on the dark skin, and his retina was probably destroyed for months. There was a great deal of pain. He cried out several times and fainted, smelling of scorched cotton and burnt hair.

They scrambled out of their cubby and stepped over the
man. Charlie picked up his gun. *Presence of mind*, he said
to himself, not knowing what to do with it.

They ran for the elevators. Just before they arrived, Charlie
detoured down the angled hall, toward the west side of the
building where Ned Crocker's office was. *They'll leave now.
They don't know where we are; they couldn't. They've lost
two people, and they'll leave.*

They slowed down in the broad cubicle space beyond the
doors. Ned Crocker's light was off, but there would be a drink
in his desk.

"Stop right there, Charlie. Don't move, Jillian. Hold the
gun by the trigger guard and put it on the floor, then kick it
toward me."

The field captain had a familiar voice.

"Turn around very slowly. Very slowly. No bows and
arrows, no flashbulbs. We're going to take a walk."

Murray Hofnung held both guns now.

"Murray. They told me you—"

"Charlie, you ruined a lot of my work, you know. You
figured out that we'd built that goddamned Dauphain at just
the wrong time. As soon as I saw your sketch, I knew
someone must have leaked it. Maybe even showed you a
photo. Or could you have seen the item, itself, at Livermore?
Do you know how much money and effort we have invested
in that project? How much seed money from contractors to
get it in place and workable before it gets disapproved out of
misguided principle? You silly man."

It fell into place in Charlie's mind, he had seen
Dauphain. Planning the X-ray laser wasn't illegal, but
building it, making it ready to deploy, planning to send it
up . . . that was illegal. But Murray! "They told me you were
dead!"

"I am. I am satisfactorily dead, ready for another new identity like Murray Hofnung. Hard to really identify a body like the one they got. And they'll find the dental records match the ones at my dentist. My former dentist."

"You're not Murray Hofnung?"

"Sure I am. I was. Now I'm not. Like I said, Charlie, you ruined a lot of my work, and you deserve worse than you're going to get. Do you know how long it took me to get into this place?"

"Yes. I hired you."

"Yes, and you kept me waiting for six months."

"Nothing was open. But you were a great researcher, Murray. We miss you. This sounds a little weird."

"Great researcher. The *Geographic* has been very backward about allowing any intelligence operatives into their staff for thirty years."

"Hell, yes. It's not journalism. It would endanger every shooter and every writer—"

"Oh, stow it. It was going to take me a few years, but we were going to have a very tight little cover, globetrotting with our camera bags and film canisters for the *National Geographic.*"

"We?"

"I would have brought in others."

"You were going to take over Stone's job?"

"No, yours."

"I didn't even know you could draw. You've got the wrong idea, Murray."

"No, we've got the right idea now. You ruined all the groundwork, and you screwed up a lot of work on Dauphain. You'll have to disappear or we'll have to set up an opera."

"An opera?" Jillian asked.

"*Romeo and Juliet*, I should think. Come along, we're

moving slowly to the elevators and down to the lower parking garage."

"How about we make a deal. I'll give you your job back and I won't tell Ruth what a shit you are."

Murray smiled, and it was this smile that turned into the worst thing Charlie had ever seen. Ned Crocker sat in a plain wooden chair at the end of the cubicles with the SharkDart from his wall. It had a one-eighth inch hypodermic needle with a trigger-collar connected to a high-pressure CO_2 flask. When a shark is hit in the midsection, the sudden flux of pressure from within usually turns the stomach inside out through the mouth. Even in a shark it is not a pretty sight, and in a former friend it is disgusting. After a few moments of confused revulsion, they all turned away.

Charlie leaned against a cubicle, his forehead on his arm. "Jesus," he said, "this is awful." And he meant that he had lost a friend twice.

Ned put his arm around Jillian, who was shaking, and they went to Ned's office and Charlie called Inspector Carlton Deauville while they opened a bottle of Bushmills.

"Guard's all right." Deauville was making more notes. "Got him with a sap and pulled him into the stairwell. Bad place for stairwells, around here. Burned fellah going to live, but he's not going to like it for a while. This other fellah, you say that's really Murray Hofnung."

"It was."

"What was he up to?"

"Long story. He wanted to be a mole, a spook in the *National Geographic*. I guess they had some odd ideas about how simple the place must be. This old place is like a monastery or the Vatican; there are so many built-up layers of tradition and obligation and procedure that it would take someone up from the bottom, like Stone, to work it. They

were going to work it like a hostile takeover, I guess. As if
the place were a computer firm or a restaurant chain,
something simple. Anyway, I ran a piece of work they were
doing outside their mole scheme, and it ruined the whole
deal for them."

"You're going to run over that slow for me another time,
right?"

"Right."

Charlie was standing on the steps of the *Geographic*. He
and Deauville stepped aside for the coroner's carts coming
up the stairs. Jillian was still being questioned. Petrov was
standing at a discreet distance, scanning the street.

"Mr. Salt, I would take it unkindly if you managed your
affairs like this too much longer, you understand? You've
told me about the man at the Natural History. We found his
revolver and silencer, and your prints on the weapon that
killed him. In the back. Still, that's an explanation for
self-defense there. Now, these folks upstairs: I got a dead
man with his eyes wide open, I don't know he's poisoned or
arrow-shot to death; I got a crispy critter can't see anything
and looks like the atom bomb went off in his drink; I got
also a real disgusting mess blown up like a bad balloon and
split out in places you tell me is the real Murray Hofnung.
That doesn't check so far, but, who knows, there is a strong
aroma of the Agencies all around this case. The heavies got
the look, they have all the tools of the trade, and the same
mushy backgrounds that won't hold up to a close look.

"Now, Mr. Salt, you may think I'm encouraging you to go
around my town and slay citizens in wild and imaginative
ways. That'd be a mistake in understanding on your part,
hear? It looks like you may just get out of this with only
about ten days of boring questioning. This happens again,

Mr. Salt, I'll know I was mistaken about you, and I'm a vain man. You know what I mean?"

Charlie, looking down the street, smelling rain, nodded. "I'd just as soon hang up my guns, Marshal. I'm not cut out for this business."

"Me neither," Deauville said as he turned to go back inside, and he sounded as if he meant it.

It began to rain lightly. Charlie pulled his coat collar up and walked down the stairs to join Petrov. As they walked toward the car and driver waiting at the alley corner, Charlie looked back and up out of habit. The Society flag still flew at half-mast for Murray.

$\triangledown$

Chapter 15

JOHN WHEELER STONE SAT behind his massive walnut desk, brooding over the layouts. He reached for a pen from the marble stand on the desk, a gift from Fidel Castro. He began to slash and circle at the gatefold of art from "Star Wars."

Charlie winced. "You really don't want to include the X-ray pop-up, John? I think it's going to be a big issue."

"Said it before. Hell, I'm about to blow this story off anyway. It's thin, just about as thin as the whole SDI idea. No, I don't want the damn pop thing. Period."

Charlie nodded. He had the idea that he was not doing his job if he didn't get thrown out of Stone's office a couple of times a year.

"This needs tightening." Stone scribbled on the layout that had taken Charlie six hours. "In other words, let's get this down to a plain spread, see? Make this spidery thing smaller, cut out these little postage stamp pictures; they're not that important. Bring this up. Okay? Let's kiss this off and get to work on something else, Charlie. Don't waste time on it. There's plenty to do. I've got about ten minutes to . . ." He rose suddenly and was gone, though Charlie could hear him shouting to his secretaries as he went.

Charlie stood in the big office and nodded grimly. A poetic

157

thought came to him; he picked up Stone's phone and used it to make his assignation. He dialed another number and spoke to Petrov. He remained standing behind the desk for a moment longer. He ran his hand over the polished surface, about twenty-five square feet of naturally shaped black walnut three inches thick. He giggled nervously and went to his office.

"Ruth, I've got to do deception, deceit, and skullduggery. Should I wear a false beard for this? Do you have a false beard available?"

"Char-lie, you already have a be-ard."

"Yes, but I could use another at times."

"You might ask Harold if you can borrow his."

"I think he's attached to it."

"Or it to him. What's going on? When are Mike and Sarah coming back?"

"Soon. A few days. Remind me to call them when I get back."

"Where are you going?"

"Doctor's appointment."

"Are you okay?"

"My gynecologist."

"Tell him to warm the speculum. Whoo!"

"I'll remember. I'll be back in an hour or so."

"What shall I tell Jil-li-an?"

"Has she called?"

"No. I just thought she might. Things look very hot and heavy, there, boy."

He shrugged. "I would wish it so, kid. No illusions, though. I may not be the cool, laid-back kind of shooter she craves."

"But Charlie," she said, putting her arm around him, "you're so . . . so . . ."

"There's the rub, kid. I'm so everything. Hard to define. So high-energy, so intense, so passionate, so embarrassing, so talkative, so intemperate, so rushing, so transparent . . . Ah shit. That lady may need to pursue someone, some tall dark type who hides behind a mysterioso screen of suave. I got no suave. Got no cool. Fresh out of laid back. I got only Groucho walks and babble and a few snappy songs. I got also to go and stop feeling sorry for myself. What do you think, Ruth?" He put on his tweed cap. "You think I ought to get an Inspector Deauville hat?"

"A what?"

"A broad-brim, snap-down, beaver-fur felt hat that can cover my eyes and my secret thoughts."

"Charlie," Ruth said, biffing him on the jaw lightly, "I like your little piggy eyes, and I like your thoughts. We all do. Don't hide them. You're not cool a bit, you dodo."

He nodded, grinning sadly, and walked down the hall with a thick layout-sized envelope under one arm. He peeked inside it on the elevator and felt guilty.

Petrov was waiting in the front lobby. "Charlie. You are looking admirably calm this morning. I admit it, you are stronger man than I thought an art director would be."

"Art directors put up with a lot. As for me, I'm about to collapse. I'm not a hit man and I'm not a field intelligence man."

"Do pretty well at both, my Charlie. A lot of American gangster in you."

"Scares me shitless. Haven't eaten in about fourteen hours. Threw up last night just out of nerves and remembering stuff." Remembering Murray as the SharkDart hit him, he had rushed into the bathroom and thrown up until there was only bile and regret coming out.

"Everyone does."

"Yeah?"

"Mmm. Look, Charlie, I have not done a lot of bad stuff,
you know. I am not a bad man, not a hoodlum. When I had
to do bad things out of necessity, still bothered my tummy.
I drink too much after bad things, also. Drank too much
after our run on the towpath. No different than you. Maybe
a little. Tough men are like the one you told me about,
Deauville. I would talk to him, if I could. He sees more than
you or I will ever see. Bad stuff by bad people. Real hoodlum
stuff.

"What's on menu, here, Charlie? Where are we going?"

They were walking toward the Farragut West Metro stop.

"This is my back-up plan, Petrov. I am about to do
something very bad, very dishonorable. I am about to become
a professional hoodlum. Do you know what a *ronin* is?"

"No. Sounds bad."

"Maybe. A ronin is a disgraced samurai, one who has no
warlord or has disobeyed his lord. He belongs to no one."

"Freedom."

"No, just alone."

The Metro closed around them, and Petrov was too busy
scanning to talk philosophy.

The platform at the L'Enfant Plaza stop was busy. Charlie
got close to Petrov. "Is there a way to tell if I'm being
followed."

"Sure. Up one level to shops and stay with me. We'll move
quick."

"You know D.C. better than I thought."

Petrov allowed himself a grin without looking at Charlie,
still scanning actively. "Washington is an old friend to me.
I was on station here several times. Good town, except in
summer."

"I like the summer."

"Lucky for you. Now we move."

On the shop level, they walked swiftly toward an exit at one end of the arcade. They walked outside and turned at the top and stopped. Charlie looked inquiringly at Petrov, but he was memorizing faces. Petrov nodded, and they plunged down into the arcade again, walking the length to another exit and stopping outside. Waiting with Petrov, Charlie shrugged his bewilderment to a passing woman, who smiled and nodded.

"Ever see *A Thousand Clowns*?"

Petrov made a negative sound as he watched the catch of faces from this troll.

"I'm going to start apologizing to everyone. I need all the forgiveness I can get. Murray apologizes to people on the street, and they forgive him, bang, just like that, out of the goodness of their hearts. Watch."

A man eating a cookie half wrapped in pale parchment came up the exit stairs. Charlie said, "Hi. Hey, I'm really sorry."

The man nodded pleasantly, crumbs falling away, and said, "Sure" around the cookie.

"Amazing," Charlie said.

"Once more, friend." They walked the length again, more slowly this time. They turned near the end and slipped between two shops, finding a door to a stairwell.

"Well?"

'One possible. Don't think so. But we don't have her on our back anymore. Where are you meeting?"

"Here in the hotel, in the restaurant at the end."

"Barley Mow would have been better. More cut up. But this is also okay. Get table not too far from door, watch kitchen entrance. I will stay in lobby."

"No lunch?"

"Hard life protecting art directors from bad guys. Should let the boogermen get you. No, not for lunch. Like you too much now, Charlie. Go become a hoodlum."

Alex Doster was on time, and faintly amused that Charlie was on time too. "A new leaf." He chuckled. They went back a long way, before Charlie had signed aboard *Geographic*. They were old, easy friends. They spent some time insulting one another and talking about women. Charlie allowed that he was seeing a shooter.

"Oh, Jesus, Charlie, don't do that. They're all inside. The lenses get in your way when you hug them. Better to hang out with a prison matron or a beautician or someone with a chance at sanity. Who is it?"

"Jillian Ansara, Dusty."

"Trouble." He shook his head.

"How's that?"

"I've met her." Dusty was in publishing. "Not just beautiful, but cute. Men fall in love with her on trains, and she travels a lot. Charlie, she'll use you and go."

"Yeah? The old question, is it better to love and lose than . . ."

"That's a stupid question. It's better to be happy. It's been a long time since you were happy. Hang out with sane women. Take care of yourself. You know what Matt says."

"Which pithy wisdom is that?"

"Never eat at a place called Mom's. Never play cards with a man called Doc. And never, never get mixed up with a woman who's more fucked up than you are."

"Look, Dusty, I came to do business. I want to give you something. Something dangerous. Someday we'll drag a case of beer to your place and I'll tell you the whole harrowing story, but right now it's just a gift. It's one of those mythical gifts from the gods that could burn. You've got to be careful, and you've got to step lively to save yourself."

"I love it. I don't care what it is. Are these nude pictures of Mrs. Gorbachev?"

"Christ, don't say that too loudly." Charlie glanced toward the lobby.

"What have you got here?"

"Lives. You've got at least seven lives in your hand. But then, a full two page spread is worth a lot of lives."

The *Geographic* layout of "Star Wars" was approved in a final picture session. Jillian explained her photos as John Wheeler Stone sat in the dark of his projection room and thumbed the advance button of the slide projector. The black-and-white layout was projected on a large television above the rear-projection slide screen. The author commented, as did the science editor and the associate editors. The small room grew warm with the thirty bodies in it, and the soft whir of the projector lulled several sleep-deprived editors to fitful napping. Researchers made notes of areas to check, issue editors noted possible difficulties of understanding, legend writers felt familiar gnawings in their stomach linings as scheduling limits were set. Two or three spreads were changed.

Charlie rose as his art spreads came up. He tried to rouse the sleeping editors as he explained the hybrid amalgam of Stone's and his own art direction. "Bear with me, now, I'm going to go very slowly and run through these things at a very basic level. It keeps me from getting confused. Stop me if I speed up, because you'll know I'm getting it wrong." He wanted to put the editors in a comfortable frame of mind, to involve them actively: We'll catch Charlie if he starts getting crazy.

He went carefully through orbital mechanics, then through the physics of chemical lasers, then he detailed the effects of particle-beam weapons. If twelve-year-olds had been allowed in the hallowed room, they would have understood the concepts. But editors are professionally stupid; they look for every possible chink in understanding, every chance for misconception or misreading. Stupidity as a science of caution, as an advanced and enlightened paranoia that only a few bright men can master. The editors asked him questions of such stunning simplicity that the answers were often difficult.

"Why wouldn't a shotgun do just as well as a million-dollar satellite, if all it does is spread debris in front of a missile?"

"Good question," Charlie said. "And you could save a lot of money if you could get an invariably accurate wing-shooter in the right orbit at the right time, and if you could persuade a Winchester pump and Peters shotshells to work at close to Kelvin zero temperatures, and if the wing-shooter didn't object to being bumped by a two-ton warhead at, say, twenty-five G's."

"These chemical lasers, they're big?"

"Generally the size of one or two semi-trailer trucks," Charlie said, reaching for simple size comparisons.

"They'd show up on radar?"

"Like a frog in a punch bowl."

"Then the other guys could shoot them down with anything."

"With a Kalashnikov that worked at low temperatures, sure."

"So what's the point?"

"I don't make policy." Charlie smiled. "I just explain technology. The going explanation is that you can maneuver

into other orbits fairly deftly if you know of a threat. They
do seem vulnerable, however."

"Who's doing the illustrations?" someone asked. The
layout sketches were Charlie's but the final illustrator had
not yet begun the job.

"Pierre Mion will do his usual crisp and prompt job."
There was a sigh of relief. Many feared that he would be
using one of his bad-boy rogue illustrators, brilliant painters
who needed handholding and Mafia persuasion to finish
work. Pierre was a complete professional, at home with
technical complexity and possessed of a graceful sense of
color and clarity. One of the rogues might bring more menace
to the illustrations, a more dramatic sense of mystery, but
Charlie had lost the desire to risk with this project. *Am I
becoming more like Harold? No, I've just been shot at
enough for one article.*

"Good," Stone said, not as a commendation or a comment
on the piece, merely as a recognition that the projection
session was over. He did not give medals. The reward for
excellence was silence and, later, perhaps, secondhand word
that he had praised it to someone else. He did not ask more
for himself.

Days of intense work on corrections gave way to the
uptake of information on other stories. Charlie sat at lunch
with Ned Crocker.

"I looked at 'Star Wars', my boy," Ned began. "Good, good
stuff."

"There's a lot to do yet. Corrections, little bits of synthesis to check. It's one thing going out with a camera and
grabbing an image, but to create the whole thing out of
information . . . drives me crazy." He was thinking about
other reasons for being crazy.

"In my years of doing pieces for the Geographic, I have
discovered this: you never finish a story, you merely abandon
it."

Charlie nodded, but he was thinking of Jillian.

The deaths in the building had caused a stir, but they
were ascribed, with Deauville's help, to simple violent burglars, and security was tightened even further. Captain Barry
was delighted. Charlie and Jillian were celebrities in the
building for days. Schneeberger demanded the arrow back
from the police and mounted it on the wall beside his
shrunken head. The furor died down.

The Sioux women descended on "Star Wars", trying to
find any small leak of truth, any contamination of bias.
Printing and Engraving toiled diligently and quietly, adjusting color and sharpening contrast in generations of proofs.
They began to ask nervously about the final art.

Charlie was distracted. *Have I changed? If Kim were here,
would she see me as different? I'm just as hyper, just as
imprudent, just as loud. Something's changed, though, inside, and she'd have to look to see. Would she? Academic,
Charlie. She's gone.*

*Someone should see. I've been through the fire and it's
burned away old deadwood. Jillian should see. Goddammit,
I deserve the effort. I try so goddamned hard at life, I rave at
it, shake it. . . .*

Then he knew he would always be the same, never the
cool and distant Gary Cooper he had wanted to be when he
was twelve. He would always be loud and furious on the
outside and shy and distant within. Would she take the
effort to look past the obvious to the calmer center? He
wanted to talk to her, convince her, show her how much he
could offer. *Charlie, for the first time in your life you're letting
someone come to you. Do you want to break that?*

Sure, I'd break that or the Pope's foot on Easter Sunday not to be lonely again. I wouldn't be lonely with Jillian.

Aw, Charlie, you haven't fallen in love with this woman after a week and a few nights in bed, have you?

No, not the nights in bed. After the danger and stress. She's graceful. Warm.

"Petrov," Charlie asked while they were eating dinner, a smoked turkey breast and tortellini with cream sauce, "are you married?"

"No. Not yet. Like to be, I think, when I rotate home. It's not good for a man to be alone. Same with you, Charlie. What about this Jillian bird?"

"Temporarily interested. She's playing."

"Cruel playing. You are interested more so?"

"More than playing, yes. Enough to look at it seriously with her. Enough to work at it a year or so to see what we have. I'm a hard worker."

"That's probably a problem right there. You won't step away and be a bad boy. Women like to get hurt, like to pursue bad boys. All kinds of women pursue me, Charlie. I'm a bad boy. I am not kind to them. You tell them your need too much, my Charlie. You're a hopeless lover, boy. Best kind of fellow, too. Hopeless. Good dinner. You cook, you're smart as hell, you're good dad, you're probably a faithful man, too. Poor booger."

"Fuck you."

"Great host, too. Listen, you think this Dauphain thing is going to work the way you got it?"

"Yes, you Bolshevik smartass. Tomorrow I meet Dusty again to go over some details."

"Where this time?

"Barley Mow."

"Okay by me."

She was filling out forms when he came in. She smiled beautifully but said nothing. He sat down across from her and recognized the forms: travel vouchers, expense vouchers, equipment requests.

He nodded to the forms. "Going on assignment?"

Smile, a nod.

"Where to?"

"Spain, the Basque country."

"A plum. Sounds great. How long will you be out of the country?"

She shrugged. "Three months at least. More, maybe. As long as the shooting weather holds up. We follow the sun." She smiled again at this lecture remark.

He looked at her framed prints on the wall: a poster from Maine, Israeli dancers by Stanfield. "I'm a foolish man."

"I know. You're a good, foolish man."

"We've been through a lot together for a couple of weeks of close acquaintance. We've shared a bed and a bodyguard for a few nights."

"Pretty exotic."

"I've tried to stay away for the last week. I figured you would call me when you were ready."

She adjusted the forms before her.

"Jillian, I'm taking a long time to say that I care for you."

She looked at him as if she were judging the light around him for a shot.

"I thought . . . I think there's enough between us to explore it seriously," he said.

She nodded sadly: Yes.

"I don't know where you are."

She shook her head. "Neither do I."

"Can you tell me where, I mean in a kind of general way, this hemisphere or that?"

"Charlie," she said, and arranged the papers again. "There's a man . . ."

"I knew about him. I thought that was over."

"I thought it was too. He's talking about getting back together. It's an old thing; it's got a lot of old emotion built into it."

"I thought it was done, pal."

"Well, it wasn't."

"He hurt you."

She shrugged.

"I'd never hurt you like that, kid."

She looked at her forms.

"He'll be in Spain?"

"Yes."

He looked at the photo of the dancers on her wall, intertwined, a complex fusion of emotion and strain and relationship.

"Tell me to wait," he said, still looking at the dancers. "Tell me, Charlie, I love you and I want you to wait for me."

"No."

"Why not?"

"It wouldn't be fair to either one of us. He has a claim on me. I love him, Charlie. I have deep feelings for you, I can't deny that, but I've got to take care of this. This is . . . always was . . . my first priority."

"Come back to me Jillian. I want you in my life." *Dammit, none of the movies end like this. She's supposed to throw herself into your arms here, right?*

"No, Charlie. It's over. Just assume it's over. No promises, no later. Over."

"I can't deal with that. I want a chance with you. I want

to be put carefully on the shelf and taken down when this
bad boy of yours finks out again."

"I can't. I do love you, Charlie, but it's not enough
sometimes."

Charlie was crying, wishing he weren't. He wanted to say,
It isn't fair, it isn't working like it should, I deserve you, I
would always. . . . But he was crying, and her face was set
like a stake driven into the ground.

"Well, my little brother," Nikolai said, "was she worth it
in experience?"

"Nothing is worth being rejected. I know she loves me,
Nick."

"No way she does not love you. But. Big but. But she loves
this other fellow first, more complicated, longer time. Roots,
Charlie. You never had a chance from instant he said to her,
'Hey, Jillian, you bitch, maybe I'll sniff around you again.'
You lose then."

"Lost before," Petrov said. "Charlie's too damn nice,
treats women too sweet. They hate that."

"Look, Charlie, you've depressed one of all-time bad boys,
Petrov. Depressed hell out of him." Nikolai spoke to him in
Russian, and Petrov replied, counting off something on his
fingers and affirming questions put to him.

"Okay. Security is tight. They have one dispirited watcher
on foot in cold. Must be small group. We have two prideful
young men eager for advancement watching him and watching back of house. Petrov, more vodka. Charlie, we're getting
drunk and talking about women. Tell you about Russian
women. What bitches! Got scars you wouldn't believe. Get
drunk and talk sad, listen to Petrov tell of his scars, too. Only
thing to do. Love you greatly, Charlie. Sorry about shooter
lady. That she should fall in love with a turnip. That she

should get her favorite finger stuck in lens of big camera. That she should remember my friend is a dear, good man."

Petrov brought in a liter of Stolichnaya, white-rimed from the freezer. He took off the cap, grinned at Nikolai and Charlie, and with Russian ceremony tossed the cap behind him into the living room. "Health," he said, and drank from the bottle.

$\triangledown$

Chapter 16

AT LAST THE TIMING was right. Dusty Doster called
Charlie and told him there would be a package waiting at
the front desk. Charlie took it from the receptionist as if it
were a letter of death from Cardinal Richelieu. He stopped
at the door to his office. "Ruth," he called, "you want to see
something . . . unusual?"

"Sure," she said peevishly. "I just lost my whole damned
schedule in the computer. Let's see whatever it is."

He sat at his desk and broke the seal, pulled it out and
laid the sheets on his desk.

"Oh, my God, this is awful," Ruth said.

Charlie pursed his lips and shook his head, "Pretty good
job, really."

"Charlie, did you have anything to do with this?"

"Yup."

"What if they find out?"

"In about ten minutes, as soon as I hit the head and wash
my face and take a few more aspirin, I'm walking up to the
Stone's office and show him myself."

"Charlie?" Christy, the department secretary, appeared
in the doorway. "There's a visitor downstairs to see you."

"Who is it?"

"Colonel William Brunzell."

"Right. Send him up, I guess."

Charlie gathered the fatal sheets into their bland envelope and waited for his visitor. He heard his footsteps approaching the door down the hall.

"Mr. Salt?"

"Right here. How do you do, Colonel? Is that right? I expected a uniform."

"Call me Bill. I'm with an intelligence group at the Pentagon, Mr. Salt. We looked at a piece you did some time ago on an X-ray laser missile." The colonel lowered his voice. "May we close this door?"

Charlie looked at him with a confusion of anger and fear and revulsion. He was a man of sixty, puffy, with protruding eyes behind glasses, slim, soft hands, and small feet in good shoes. His navy blazer carried a bullion crest on the pocket and what may have been gold buttons. His shirt was a broadcloth blue awning stripe, and his tie was a warm red. Could this neat, tailored bureaucrat be the head of the intelligence group that had tried to kill him? His voice was soft, southern, and his manner gentlemanly.

"May I ask, Colonel, how far your interests extend? How important is this X-ray missile concept to you?"

"Oh, very important, indeed, Mr. Salt. We would go to great lengths to protect our country's interest in this matter."

"To lengths outside the law?"

"There are advantages to a group like ours, Mr. Salt. We operate in a fairly loose-jointed way with few chartered restrictions. The gray area of necessity where the law ends is our natural habitat."

"We're sitting in my office at my desk. Let's be frank, Colonel. . . ."

"Bill."

"Yes, let's be frank. Are you threatening me?"

"My information is that you have had several close calls in the last few weeks. Threats would roll off your ducklike back, Charles. No, I'm here to talk business. You might be surprised to learn how much money is involved in the prototype of a missile like the one you've stolen."

"Not stolen. I figured out the details without any outside aid, with only unclassified sources. The name of the project is the only classified piece of information I copped, and that from an indiscreet physicist at Lawrence Livermore where I think I saw the warhead or the prototype. Not my fault."

"The physicist has been censured. Security has tightened. But we believe you may have had help from another, more resourceful intelligence-gathering agency."

"The KGB."

"Yes." The Colonel rubbed his soft hands, as if they were cold.

"The KGB, through an old friend who is not my boss, not my master, protected me and my children from my own government. Nice fellahs. Now, what in hell do you want here?"

"Cooperation. At a price. A fair price running to, let us say, five undeclared figures."

"You should have brought this up weeks ago. Damn, I could use that kind of money for the kids' college fund."

"What do you mean, 'weeks ago'?"

"Here, Colonel. These proof sheets may be of interest to you." He opened the envelope again and spread them out. The colonel examined them.

"Ah. This is disappointing. It seems we have nothing more to speak of, Mr. Salt. You are a foolish and a resourceful man. If, in the future, we can work with you rather than against you . . ."

"Yes, sir. If your little group survives this. Colonel, may I bring my children home?"

"You must understand that there is nothing personal in—"

"Don't tell me that. Don't tell me bullets and knives and secrets aren't personal. Tell me you're sorry, you slimy son of a bitch. Tell me you're sorry and shouldn't have done any of this, that it was a moral lapse. Tell me you'll do penance by becoming a Buddhist monk and traveling the country with a robe and a bowl. But don't be polite. I'm just an explainer, Colonel. I explain complicated things to eleven million people every month. I'm also a father. Those are a couple of difficult jobs made harder by being shot at and threatened. Oh, just go away."

"I'm sorry, Mr. Salt. Yes, by all means. Bring your children home. There is nothing more to threaten you for. You don't know the damage you've done. If you did, if you know how powerfully you are jeopardizing the safety of your country, you might feel very differently about this and about my people."

"Go back to your people, Colonel. The safety of the country is down at the Archives. They guard it pretty well, the Constitution, but they can never guard against your brand of psychotic patriotism. You're dangerous, Colonel. I hope they get you and your people."

"You don't know how useful we are, Mr. Salt. They may censure us, but only for allowing you to interfere, and for allowing the KGB to win."

"Win, lose. Hell, Colonel, is it that simple? Go back to your people."

He walked into Stone's office.

"Charlie, I've got an idea about the December cover."

"John, I've got to show you something. You're not going to like it."

Stone put down his sheaf of papers.

"Right off the bat, John, I'm not the mole."

"What?"

There was one issue that carried more weight than any other at *Geographic*. It was a constant source of embarrassment, and yet it went on year after year. Somewhere in the organization there was a mole, a leak to *Geographic*'s smaller, quicker competitor.

Charlie took the sheets out of the large, manila envelope and laid them sequentially, carefully on the coffee table before Stone's couches. They were final proof sheets, ready to go. A full story, "SDI's Galaxy of High-Tech Stars," with Charlie's spread on the pop-up X-ray laser missile, Dauphain. The sheets were set in a familiar Baskerville display and text type, and each was marked, *Smithsonian Magazine*.

John Wheeler Stone looked at the sheets silently for thirty seconds. Then he said, very quietly, "'Get the fuck out of here. Leave those."

He started back to his desk for his phone.

"John, you'd better let me tell you how this came about. It's complicated, hard to believe, and it may be to our advantage in the long run."

Stone glared at him. He didn't reply, but made two calls. The two doors at opposite ends of his office opened at the same time. Sean McCorley, the associate editor, came through one, and Richard Bellweather, the president and chairman of the board of the National Geographic Society, came through the other.

"Here," Stone said, and pointed at the sheets.

"Christ." Sean held both hands out to the display. "The

whole goddamned story, including Charlie's pop-up. How in God's name did they get this stuff?"

"It's the mole," Bellweather said grimly. He had been editor-in-chief before Stone. "It's the damn mole."

"I gave it to them," Charlie said, with as strong a voice as he could muster. *'Tis a far, far better thing I do than I have ever done before. 'Tis a far, far better world I go to . . . Ronald Coleman has a stronger voice for things like these.*

"Do you know what you're saying?" Bellweather said.

"I think so. This spread on the pop-up? Corporal Wheeler was killed for it. I figured out so many of the details and probably *saw* the son of a bitch—accidentlly, at Livermore so the layout was too accurate. The intelligence organization that was underwriting its illegal development began to think I knew just how far they'd gotten. They tried to kill me three or four times because of it. Some friends protected me, and I had to send my children off to protect them."

McCorley was agitated. "Are Sarah and Mike safe now? Are they all right?"

"Yes, they're okay. The three men who came in here a couple of weeks ago and chased Jillian Ansara and me weren't burglars. They were hit men from the intelligence group. One of them was Murray Hofnung."

"But he died. He was dead by then."

"The body was a plant. Murray was to be another kind of mole, a real intelligence mole who would use *Geographic* as a cover."

"We can't have that. We won't have that at all." It was Bellweather who was agitated now.

"I'll give you the name of the colonel in charge. I think some of our board members swing enough weight to have him up by his heels. I hope so. In any case, John," Charlie addressed his warlord directly, "the only thing I could do to

get myself and my family out of danger was to publish the
thing. I did my best to sell the layout, but you didn't want
it in our coverage."

"Why didn't you tell me?"

"Would it have made a difference?"

"No."

"I knew that. And I knew that's not the way we work."

"But you gave it to the competition."

"I checked first. They already had a story on SDI rolling,
ready to go months before ours would be out. But it wasn't
as good; it needed something new. I had something for
them."

"You made their story."

"I also made a deal."

"It's a pretty good story alright." McCorley was looking it
over.

"What did you get?"

"I got the mole."

Stone, Bellweather, and McCorley stopped, exchanged
looks, and looked at Charlie. "Who is it?" Stone asked
roughly.

"First, it isn't me, goddammit. This place is my home, my
loyalty lies here. John, you're my editor. I like what I do, and
I do it well."

Stone nodded, a major plaudit.

"If you want me to go, I will. I'd like to stay."

"You go, I'll break your leg," Stone said. "You've got plenty
to do here. Now, who is the mole?"

"It's Peter Baron, one of the issue editors. He's been having
a long affair with one of the text editors at *Smithsonian*."

"But he's married to one of our people."

"Nice fellah, no?" Charlie commented with some venom.

"Fire his ass," Bellweather said.

"I wouldn't. Not right away," Charlie said. "Most of the folks at *Smithsonian* don't know I've found out about him. Use him for a few months. Feed him the wrong information. Done all the time in the intelligence world." He said intelligence with a new emphasis. "Don't give him a raise, don't give him a promotion. Eventually, you can confront him with what you know and turn him, use him against them, use the threat of a bad recommendation."

"Let's just fire him." Bellweather shoved his hands in his pockets.

'Let's take him out in the courtyard and shoot him." Sean McCorley's Irish answer.

"Let's have a drink."

They opened Stone's bar and sat down with drinks around the layout. "Look at this shit," Stone said. He reached for his pen and began to circle and slash at the layouts.

$\triangledown$

Chapter 17

CHARLIE SALT WAS DREAMING. *Pendragon* was under full sail, coming out of Tenant's Harbor, Maine. Charlie was giving the main downhaul a final tug. The sails were set and drawing beautifully, bright with clean, warm sunshine. There must have been a rain to wash them down. The brightwork seemed to hum with a golden glow in the Maine light, and the brass must have been polished that morning. The lobster pots leaped past, blue and yellow and red and chartreuse green and international orange and any color the lobstermen wanted, like crystals of pure sea elements. The land was deep green with gray ledges and russet beds of weed. In his dream, he looked at how the lobster buoys were streaming and saw the tide was falling. The lighthouse and diaphone on Southern Island gleamed with the same intense light and seemed to pump urgency into the dream. Charlie touched the sail and felt its tautness, the live power of a dancer's thigh. He moved aft.

Jillian was at the wheel with a cup of coffee in her hand. She smiled at him and nodded, assenting to something he did not understand, then she looked forward to her steering. What was she doing on *Pendragon*? He seemed to be on a track, doing things that were preordained and separate from his wishes. He stooped to the transom and pulled in the dinghy from where it waited, balanced on the quarter wake. He coiled its long painter as it came to him. In his dream, it rocked in the slick swirling water under the transom. The oars were lashed to the thwarts, and their varnish gleamed in the dream light.

He stepped into the dinghy. He knew he was to let go, but he didn't want to. Jillian turned to him, and her smile had turned sad. Let go, Charlie, the smile said. He looked forward to the companionway and saw Kim's sweet, freckled face, grave and mischievous at the same time, coming up. Let go, Charlie, the face said. He glanced to starboard and saw they were almost abreast of Southern Island. He didn't know how to stay on a boat of spirits, but he knew how to board a dinghy. *Do what you know, Charlie*, he said to himself, *and let go*.

He pulled the painter forward, swung out over the stern pulpit, and landed crouched amidship at the dinghy's center of balance, still holding *Pendragon's* toerail. His weight slewed the little boat under him. One hand was busy with the slipped half-hitches that held the oars, and then he had them canted in their oarlocks. *Let go, Charlie*.

He watched his hand release its grip. He crouched as the transom glided away and the dinghy caught the wake.

He swung the dinghy's bow toward the village with one oar, and then he was looking aft to *Pendragon* bounding away. There was no one on deck. The wheel was locked, and the sails were taking it east. It looked as if it would just clear Two Bush Island and sail on, almost forever.

He rowed. He passed lobster pots and, once, the body of a gray-haired man in a tweed jacket being taken out with the tide. It did not bother him in the dream, because the sea cleans itself. Toward the east, he saw a spout and the tail

lob of a blue whale in the Gulf. The light was flat and strong
and made the sails of the retreating sailboat vibrate in his
sleeping eyes.

Charlie Salt woke. It was very quiet. He looked at his
clock. He had slept a long time. The room was chilly, and
his big robe felt good. He looked out the window: the black
of elms and the white of a new snow. The autumn was over.

He knocked softly at Sarah's door and came in to a muffled
"Hmumph."

"Hey, kid. Snow."

"I know. I got up to go to the bathroom, and it was
snowing." Her eyes were still closed. "Will there be school?"

"There would be in Vermont."

"How about the District, Dad?" The regal tones of a
noblewoman dealing with her halfwit gardener crept in.

"Here, my dear, they think of snow as a judgment, an
infernal punishment sent by dark contingents of unrecon-
structed Vermont people who are still angry about the Civil
War."

"Ohmygod, you are so tiresome in the morning. I swear
to God, really."

"I'll go."

"No." A small girl's voice and a sudden capture of his
hand. "Talk to me. I missed you, Daddy."

"How is everything in Bath?"

"I didn't meet a single person, and no one, I swear this is
true, not one person listens to music unless they're on an
elevator, and there are no elevators in Bath. I don't want to
talk about Bath. Mike can tell you everything. He was all
over the river in this stupid boat. He is such a retard, I swear
to God."

"Was he good?"

"His table manners are just like, I swear, a hog's, really."

"Were John and Karen offended?"

"No. Not one bit. I ate like a real polite person, and Mike just ate everything, just stuffed it in and told them how good it was and made awful noises. They loved him. He's disgusting. He's cute; I love my brother. But we've got to do something about his table manners. I hit him one night. I swear, he needed it, really. I just hit him."

"With what?"

"With a quahog shell. Right on the head. He was acting so disgusting."

"I don't know, Sadie. Hitting a fellow diner with a quahog isn't exactly good dinner etiquette either."

"I know, I know. What about Jillian? She's not coming back, is she?"

"Kid, you're going to have to put up with having the toilet seat up a while longer."

"Why isn't she? She likes you, I know she does."

"I think she does, yeah. But she's got another guy, and it's a long-standing thing with her. She's got to try to make it work. That's the way she is. Besides, I'm just not her cuppa."

"You are too. You're cute, too, Poppa."

"Well, pal, I'm also wrapped up in my own stuff. I'm very intense. I burn people out. I go too fast." He was looking out at the bare branches through the window. "It would be tough for anyone like Jillian to share with me. I may not be very good at sharing, though I would like to try. Your mum and I, we had troubles with the same stuff. But I was younger and hadn't been through as much. Maybe now . . ."

"You've got us."

"Yes'm."

"That's not enough, though, is it?"

"It'll do for now."

"Will Jillian ever come back?"

"I don't know. Sure, if she were smart she'd hike back this way and try the water. A lot of men fall in love with a woman like Jillian, though. She looks softer than she is. But maybe she'll remember what she's left here. I don't know. I'm a fool when it comes to women, kid."

"You are a real retard, Dad. What about Uncle Nick?"

"Wednesday night at the Chowder and Marching Society. Nikolai is anxious to see you guys. Also, Petrov will be there with a lady from *Geographic* he picked up while he was waiting for me outside the building."

"Is he nice to women?"

"He's nice to you."

"Yes."

"He's a bad boy with women. I'm taking lessons."

"Are we okay now? Is anyone watching us?"

"We're fine now, sweets."

Mike was still asleep. His room smelled faintly like a rabbit hutch. One foot was out. It had a Band-Aid on it. His face was totally untroubled clear, *tabula rasa*.

The snow was coming again. Charlie stood at Mike's window and watched it. *I have done wicked things. I was protecting myself, but I must recognize my part in them and live the wickedness away.*

And I have failed. I have failed at presenting my information in the forum I chose. I have failed at keeping my information on a professional level; I needed the damned KGB.

I have failed to hold a woman I love. Maybe I should have used the KGB for that. Or the Mossad. Or the Vatican or anyone else.

What now? Well, Salt, you've got a story load of sixteen

articles to explain to eleven million people. As Stone says, time to finish up and move on to something else. There's plenty to do.

Charlie ran his hand across his beard and turned away from the window. He bent down beside Mike and checked carefully for evidence of squirt guns or Walther PP's or curare-tipped arrows or flint spears. None.

He stood up and raised his eyebrows. "Aha, Schottsie!" He became Middle-European. "You become one of the Undead!" He pounced on the defenseless boy's tummy and tickled him awake.

If you have enjoyed this book and would like to receive details of other Walker Mystery-Suspense novels, please write for your free catalog:

Walker and Company
720 Fifth Avenue
New York NY 10010